'Aching  olitical
satire . . .   times . . .
delicious   ly funny.'

'*Enter the Aardvark* sizzles with uproarious fun,
from its snout to the sting in its tale.'
INDEPENDENT

'What begins as a topical takedown of the
American political system deepens into a hugely
enjoyable romp through history.'
OBSERVER

'It's a long time since I have enjoyed a novel so
much. Fresh, witty and smart, it also has a heart.'
KATE ATKINSON

'You're in for a treat . . . Completely insane
but utterly hilarious.'
JOHN BOYNE

'Fresh, astute and mouthwateringly sharp, this
is a rare thing; a political satire that tugs on the
heartstrings in unconventional ways.'
IRISH TIMES

'Jessica Anthony's *Enter the Aardvark* was
exactly the smart, funny and poignant pick-me-up
that I needed . . . riotously entertaining.'
I-NEWS

'Mischievously zoological and darkly
satirical – a brilliant novel.'
JOHN IRONMONGER

www.penguin.co.uk

Enter
the
Aardvark

JESSICA ANTHONY

doubleday

TRANSWORLD PUBLISHERS
Penguin Random House, One Embassy Gardens,
8 Viaduct Gardens, London SW11 7BW
www.penguin.co.uk

Transworld is part of the Penguin Random House group of companies
whose addresses can be found at global.penguinrandomhouse.com

Penguin
Random House
UK

First published in Great Britain in 2020 by Doubleday
an imprint of Transworld Publishers
Paperback edition published 2021

A CIP catalogue record for this book
is available from the British Library.

ISBN
9781784165185

Typeset in 11/14.5pt Fairfield Light by Jouve (UK), Milton Keynes.
Printed and bound in Great Britain by Clays Ltd, Elcograf S.p.A.

The authorized representative in the EEA is Penguin Random House Ireland,
Morrison Chambers, 32 Nassau Street, Dublin D02 YH68

Penguin Random House is committed to a sustainable
future for our business, our readers and our planet. This book
is made from Forest Stewardship Council® certified paper.

To Thomas Shearman Anthony
and Susan Terrell Anthony

One of the inevitablest private miseries is this multitudinous efflux of oratory and psalmody from the universal human throat; drowning for the moment all reflection whatsoever, except the sorrowful one that you are fallen in an evil, heavy-laden, long-eared age, and must resignedly bear your part in the same.

Thomas Carlyle, 1850

Enter
the
Aardvark

– a whirling mass of vapors is unhinged, shooting through outer space for an infinity until it collides with an ellipsis which *does not let go,* and after another infinity, the vapors boil into fire clouds, trapped by gravity, turning and returning until the boiling clouds, accepting fate, cool into a single mantle which cracks open in places, and here comes the lava, expanding, but there are also places where the expanding lava cannot escape and so it (the lava) pushes itself against itself and ta-da: *mountains,* new vapor rises up through the surface of the mantle, hitting the air, and it is all at once *water, big water,* and this *big water* hits the *hot lava,* steam shoots up, pluming, and it's these watery plumes rising and falling ad nauseam that birth *the oceans,* and within *the oceans* are vast trenches paralleled by islands, which are cool rock formations from the hot lava varietals sludging obscenely over the mantle, itself now a whole globe of unmappable graywacke and chert, and the sun shines upon these waters until, in the shallowest banks, atolls and shelves, tumbling in the warm current, here come the flagellates, the plankton and phytoplankton, all tense, innumerous, ticking and rolling the floor-bottom, which is coated in algae and lampshells and pouchy glass sponges until here come the copepods, krill and medusae, the crab larvae, the pteropods, salps and heteropods, and the worms – my god, the arrow worms, something must be done about the freaking arrow worms – so enter the squirrelfish, enter the mantis shrimp, the flat/lantern/hatchet fish, enter the miniature squid, and some grow tails, and all have shells and mouths, they swallow everything, fattening into fish, and these plumpy fish grow long, swimmy, they shake the oceans *into a state*, and some of these fish hanging out at the edges of some of these pools are bumping their snouts into the earth, they want to dry off, go upland, and Lo, here begins the Great Creep, and will you look at them there ectothermic tetrapod vertebrates *go*!

All hail the Devonian nerds! The tiktaaliks and tulerpetons tossing back their flat heads, fuffing oxygen up through their watery tubes, eventually shedding their gills for skin, for open air, and still *another* infinity must pass as these miserable vertebrates *scha-lump* around the shifting plates until they at last settle the Karoo beds of southern Africa as bent-legged, flared-elbowed reptilians all mastering the art of double articulation, their planes of movement align, they hasten toward quickening until in their skulls a second bony palate is formed, foreshadowing the near-complete separation of food, of air, these therapsid temporal openings are migrating toward the top of the skull, and here's the sagittal crest, the brain case and rostrum, they are the virgin class Mammalia, within which not long after emerges a clade of afrotherian mini-beasts, litters of sengis and tenrecs, shrews and hyraxes. Their tiny snouts toughen. Soft hides go *real thick* as the fur thins, showing off the tough hide, which is pinkish-yellow in hue, gleaming under the sun, and what's there to eat, there's nothing to eat, *we must find something to eat,* and so they dig. A hoof appears.

But the hoof is lousy at digging. It cleaves thrice and *voilà!* Lose the pollex, enter the claws, each a thick spoon. Enter the ears, long, soft and tubular. Enter the buccal snout, twice as long as a pig's, half as long as an anteater's, but it is not an anteater's; this particular snout holds nine olfactory bulbs, best of anybody out there on the grasslands, stampeding the hot, bitchy savannah – and after another infinity, through the parallel evolution of a far less sturdy mammal, Modern Man, one of whom goes by the name Sir Richard Ostlet (but what are names), and Sir Richard Ostlet assigns to them in 1875 (but what is time) the order Edentata, 'without teeth,' before realizing he's wrong; the creature is, in fact, Tubulidentata. The teeth are there, at the back, by the throat. These dentine tubes, they serve the tongue, which is itself slender, protractile, and covered with a thick, viscous substance to which ants and termites clawed up from the ground will all, from here on out, helplessly adhere –

'Enter *Orycteropus* into the log,' Ostlet tells his assistant as he examines the claws. 'That's from the Greek. Do you know what it means?'

The young man shakes his head.

'Digging footed,' says Ostlet. 'With the ears of a rabbit and snout like a pig. But what to call it?' He begins pacing. 'Enter "the hare pig." The ears and snout tell us they're guided by hearing and smell— No, wait. Enter "the ant bear,"' he says.

But that's still not right.

He asks one of the African hunters what they call these beasts.

'Aarde vaarke,' the hunter says, and the hunter, black and handsome, does not know that his people adopted the word centuries ago from Dutch colonists as he points: 'Earth pig.'

Ostlet nods vigorously. 'Enter "the aardvark,"' he says, which the young assistant, a student of his in the Department of Naturalism at the University of Edinburgh, obediently enters.

1

IT IS AUGUST. CONGRESS IS in recess. You are not in recess. You are running a reelection campaign for the First Congressional District in Virginia. Your opponent's name is Nancy Beavers, and you have made up your mind that from here on out there will be no more days off. If you are going to lose your job, it is not going to be to a woman. Not a woman named Nancy. Not a woman named *Nancy. Fucking. Beavers.*

So you had no intention of taking today off, but today there's a heat wave. Grids are out all over the city. Your grid is one of the ones that are out.

The A/C is not working. The internet is not working. The TV is not working. Nothing is working. You are not working.

You are reposed upon a Victorian sofa the color of canaries that your assistant purchased for you three days ago at a street antique fair for $1900, flipping through the book *Images of Greatness: An Intimate Look at the Presidency of Ronald Reagan* until you find what you're looking for: a photograph of the Gipper reclined upon a canary-yellow velvet Victorian sofa.

Important-looking papers cross his chest.

You have looked at this photograph many times – it is the reason why you purchased this sofa, and now that you have it, you are lying on the exact same sofa in the exact same position as Ronald Wilson Reagan.

You turn the page.

There is Dutch, the Gipper, on his ranch, riding a horse chased by piebald foxhounds, the paunch of his stomach outlining a lightweight denim cowboy shirt, and you bought that exact same shirt at the exact same antique fair, and how the flaps of his tan riding pants do crest the tops of his riding boots, you think, and consider sending your assistant to return to the fair to seek out those boots, when the doorbell rings.

Your doorbell is not a buzzer, it's something more ancient. Like from the Eighties. You wonder who it could be because no one ever comes to your door. Everyone always comes to your office. Then you wonder how the doorbell is working when nothing else is. The doorbell, you realize, is not attached to the grid.

This freaks you out.

It could be Rutledge or Olioke, you think, the two con-gressmen who stay with you during the week in the extra rooms of your townhouse near the Capitol while Congress is in session, but that's highly unlikely: Representative William 'Billy' Rutledge (D) is back on his farm with his wife and five sons. He left two days ago and won't be back 'til September. Representative Solomon 'Sammy' Olioke (R) is at some cottage with his wife and five daughters. Some crappy cottage by some crappy lake, and Olioke leaves his crap everywhere in your townhouse, he's crappy at governing, he's from Rhode Island, he's been reelected four times, so even though he's a Republican, you kind of hate Olioke.

The doorbell rings again.

You have no wife, no children. You, like Representative Rutledge, are young, white and handsome, however you are a bachelor. You are fine with this. This was the hallmark of your first campaign (this and abortion). It's how people know you. But now that you are facing reelection, your aides are not fine with this: your Favorability Rating is currently holding steady at 52%, which, although good, is not as good as it could be, and as of late your aides have been telling you to Find A Wife.

If you Find A Wife, they say, your Favorability Rating will improve, because although you are neck and neck with Nancy Fucking Beavers, a middle-aged woman with an ass like two neighborly cast-iron skillets who wears these unbelievable pantsuits – Nancy Fucking Beavers is not fucking single. She has fucking children. Your platform is Bachelor and her platform is Children, and you are trying to wrap your brain matter around the fact that many people who should constitute *your* electorate will actually trust Nancy Fucking Beavers more than they trust you simply because she has *chil*dren, roundly discarding the fact that her only experience in government is losing a local mayoral campaign by a hair, when the doorbell rings a third time.

You go upstairs. You put on your bathrobe.

Your bathrobe is navy blue with red piping and cost $398. It is monogrammed 'APW' in Chancery on the breast pocket and is Egyptian cotton from Bill Blass, Ronald Reagan's favorite designer. There is a picture of Reagan wearing the bathrobe in *Images of Greatness,* from when he got shot, and you always feel pretty good wearing the bathrobe, which is why, even though it's so hot out, you put on the bathrobe.

You wear an oxford underneath. Like Reagan. Even after he got shot, he wore an oxford underneath.

You are less of a man than Ronald Reagan, you know this, but no one will ever be able to say about you that your goals were not lofty, you think as you return downstairs and open the door.

1875

Sir Richard Ostlet, a fifty-year-old, richly mustachioed zoological naturalist, is in the Karoo beds of southern Africa, an area that will one day be known as Namibia, searching for strange mammals to bring home to Britain, and these particular mammals, the aardvarks, despite the fact that they have lived for several thousand millennia before Richard Ostlet, to him, fit the bill.

They look like some kind of *joke,* Ostlet thinks, like some kind of *accident,* part rabbit, part pig, or even part kangaroo, but in reality, the aardvark is none of these things; nor is it strange to the two African hunters working for Ostlet who kill these beasts regularly, for sport and/or meat, and who are, at this moment, presenting him with three high-quality specimens rooted out from their long, sandy tunnels last night.

Of the three specimens, one immediately stands out to Ostlet. Marvelously humpbacked, profoundly clawed, she is the oldest and therefore largest of the three, and reminds the naturalist of something but he cannot say what. For whatever it is, it's neither the hypotrichous skin, yellow-pink, nor the four earth-colored limbs – plantigrade at the front, digitigrade at the back – and it's not the round, wrinkled scalp common to Ungulata and other hooved mammals, nor the ears, folded like silk, nor the stretched piggy snout with its coarse whiskers that cluster the nostrils, bridge the nose and even sprout from the cheeks – it's something in the eyes, he thinks, which are soft, long-lashed, making her expression *flirtatious yet noble,* like an intelligent dog, and as the others leave Ostlet to dine in a nearby tent, he continues to stare at the dead aardvark, surprising himself when he sees in the face a kind of melancholy, he hasn't felt this sad in years, and the burden is so sudden, so heavy, his first instinct is to share it, to split it with someone.

But there is no one there with whom to split it.

For Ostlet cannot say to his assistant 'enter the melancholy, like a reckoning' or 'enter the malaise, like a frozen ground-swell,' and so: a plan is formed. This aardvark is selected. The carcass will be preserved for the boat back to England, and the skin, skeleton, notes and all sketches, will be delivered to Ostlet's close friend, the taxidermist Mr Titus Downing of Royal Leamington Spa, the only man in the world, Sir Richard Ostlet believes, who might actually be able to do the aardvark justice.

The aardvark will make it to Leamington Spa.

Ostlet will not.

Late that night, the man, who is newly married to a slim, pretty botanist named Rebecca, and who, mere months ago, signed a lease on a lovely new flat on the lovely Gloucester Walk between Holland and Hyde, two of the loveliest parks in London; the man who participates in all the social 'field clubs' such as the Midland Union, the Yorkshire Naturalists' Union, the prestigious Cotteswold Club, which serves its members seedcake and champagne; the man who, up to this moment, has been considered by all he knows to be wholly openhearted, privileged with a preternaturally optimistic disposition, one he has enjoyed since his youth, will find himself awake in the dark tent in Africa, driven out of his dreams.

Richard Ostlet will rise from his cot and root through his small wooden cabinet of gear, which is five rows of cork-lined drawers, each papered and stuffed with the *accoutrements* of any naturalist: the chalk tins and marking pins, the white gum erasers, round prickly sponges, lidded glass jars, brown bottles of chloroform, and above all, numerous white lumps of camphor, which are necessary for the preservation of the specimens; and this is an irony Ostlet does not consider as he removes the camphor lumps from their drawers, grabs a bottle of whisky, and, one by one, ingests them, pill-like, to his death.

∽

The man at the door is wearing a purple and black FedEx uniform. He is carrying a FedEx clipboard and behind him, a white FedEx truck hums in the heat. It's FedEx.

'Representative Wilson?' he says.

'Yes,' you say.

'Sign here,' he says.

The man is an average height, a bit on the round side maybe, and sports a long brown beard, these funny-looking thick eyeglasses, and you will swear that these are the only details about him you are able to recall when you are seated in front of a congressional committee for your impeachment hearing – but that has not happened yet. That will not happen for another six weeks. Right now your only concern is the very large cardboard box with your name on it, which is standing, upright, behind the FedEx man. There is no return address.

'What is it,' you say. 'Who's it from.'

The FedEx man does not answer. He checkmarks the clipboard, walks quickly back to the delivery truck and climbs into the driver's seat. He drives away.

In the playground across the street where local children go to scream, a chubby black boy stands alone, apart from the others. He is not screaming. He is watching you. He wants to see what's in the box, and you can hardly blame him: the box is, after all, like, *really big*. It takes up your whole stoop.

You try and lift it. You cannot lift it.

The boy watches as you try and lift it.

How the *hell* did the FedEx man carry this thing to

your stoop by himself, you wonder, and decide that you need to work out more. Stop eating carbs.

Your assistant, Barb Newberg, eats carbs all the time, but she doesn't like to eat carbs by herself, so she hauls into your office endless plastic bins of Panera. Oily danish and muffins. Barb and her carbs. Like so many middle-aged women you know, Barb Newberg confuses kindness and gluttony, and it's really time for a new secretary, you think as you examine the box, which is certainly big and certainly heavy and all blank but for the taped seams, your name and your address in Foggy Bottom, which is 2486 Asher Place in the fine and fair city of Washington, DC.

You stop for a second and consider: maybe you *shouldn't* bring something inside the house without knowing its makeup or origin (the post-9/11 Amerithrax scare when you were an intern has never quite left you), and that is why, standing out here in your bathrobe on the landing of Asher Place Townhouses across the street from the city playground with a chubby black boy staring at you now *very intently* on one of the hottest days of the year, you leave the box on your stoop, hustle inside to the kitchen and rummage the drawers until you find what you're looking for: a knife, and it is a small, rust-dotted paring knife belonging to Olioke, which you carry in one hand as you return to the box.

You pare the seam. You look inside as the boy, unsupervised, crosses the street and walks up behind you.

'What's *that*,' he says.

The boy climbs up your stoop uninvited and watches

respectfully as you stab two messy slits into each side. His patience, he thinks, will be rewarded. It's only fair.

But life isn't fair.

By slipping your hands through the slits, you create makeshift handles, and, in this manner, sort of tug the giant box inside, into your living room, ignoring the look on the boy's face as you gently close the door on him, in silence.

You open the box and immediately recall from fifth grade a picture book called *Mammals of Africa:* how in the book there was a beast that looked like an anteater; how when the teacher called on you, you talked so confidently about the anteater and were mortified when the teacher scolded you when you were finished talking for not getting it right – it was no *anteater* because *anteaters* were in *South America,* she said, and your class had been studying *Africa,* and she held up the book and pointed at the title *Mammals of Africa* – and the teacher, Ms Sline, who had spent one year living in London with her fiancé before he left her, who still spoke with a fake British accent and even, occasionally, adopted dumb British slang into her speech, barely opened her mouth when she said the word to you, and when she asked you to spell it, you spelled it like you heard it, and that is how the other children came to calling you Odd Fuck all year – but it is not solely because of this memory that you know the gigantic taxi-dermied beast in your living room is an aardvark; you know it's an aardvark because that is what Greg Tampico told you the first time he finished sucking your cock.

∽

· 15 ·

The address for Titus Downing's taxidermy shop is 24 Victoria Terrace in Royal Leamington Spa, and it's the one on the corner, directly across from the All Saints' Church, unmissable for the twelve heads of adult white-tailed stags, full-antlered, that hang outside the shop where perhaps a long awning should be.

Titus Downing: slim, forty and wan, is one of England's premier taxidermists, the only taxidermist, in fact, who has received a royal warrant from Queen Victoria. In 1875, Downing is enjoying a bit of local fame, for he has recently stuffed, shaped and mounted the skin of a nearly two-ton African giraffe which has been purchased by Leicester's New Walk Museum and now greets museum-goers in its Grand Hallway. A reporter at the *Evening Standard* enthused, 'This giraffe is so lifelike that upon Viewing, one expects the giraffe's legs to nimbly walk off their mount!' and, after the giraffe, traveled by train, via Birmingham to Leamington, demanding to know Downing's secret: how was it *possible* to make a dead thing look so truly alive? 'It is like *magic*,' he said, and Titus Downing, who believes the art of the taxidermist is not all that different from the art of the magician, replied thusly:

'You are asking me how to create beauty. The secret lies only in displaying beauty truthfully to life. The beauty must be recognized for its own sake, even by the unscientific. This is the case I advocate, and the end I have in view,' and it was the best way Downing could explain to the man that taxidermy is not about death, it's about *life*. It's rebirth, it's *religion*, and every carcass that falls into

Downing's hands is *actually reborn;* it is Christ beckoning Lazarus to come out, *out* of his cave.

It began over two decades ago, in 1851, when the young Titus Downing attended the Great Exhibition in London. He paid no attention to the intricate glasswork of the grand Crystal Palace or the largesse of the Koh-i-Noor diamond or Brady's daguerreotypes or the tempest prognosticator with its storm-sniffing leeches; Downing's gaze was fixed solely upon forty-two-year-old Charles Darwin, there to explain the work of every taxidermist on display. Darwin had practiced the art of taxidermy on the *Beagle* but learned it at Edinburgh from John Edmonstone, a freed Guianese slave who made his own living this way: teaching taxidermy.

The Guianese, Darwin said, predominantly Hindu and Jain, knew the art of rebirth better than anyone. The *atman* or *jiva,* they believe, the immortal life-essence of each living being, is intrinsically pure, everlasting, and ever since knowing this, Titus Downing has been at practice, re-creating the appearance of a creature's 'moving skin' to awaken its precise *jiva,* and although he is not the first British taxidermist to stuff a giraffe, because the giraffe Downing has stuffed so honestly bears its *jiva,* he agreeably intuits that the reporter at the *Evening Standard* and so many others, they may well be correct: he is *uniquely* skilled (perhaps, even, the best at his craft), so it is not in the least bit surprising to Titus Downing that his talent has reached a state of refinement never before reached by the Great Exhibitors, nor by Darwin, nor even, perhaps, by the freed Guianese slave.

Yet Downing himself is not rich. He is not even that popular. This is because his work, he believes, is widely misunderstood.

Women in particular, though many men too, upon hearing his profession, enjoy regaling him with stories about the Sussex shop of the wealthy Mr Walter Potter and his 'Museum of Curiosities,' and Titus Downing of Leamington Spa has no time for people who think that he does what Walter Potter is doing.

Walter Potter – the very name casts a spoil upon the tongue! – *Walter Potter,* who anthropomorphizes any number of little beasts into obscene human tableaux: gerbils sipping tea, rabbits at cards, kittens wearing miniature wedding gowns, all of which the public adores?

Walter Potter is the reason why the public's attention matters not to Titus Downing.

Downing's method, if one can call it a method, is supplication. It's prayer. For only by exercising total humility, he believes, can one fully invoke the desires of another. To understand how a creature moves, you have to know what a creature *wants,* and it is in this way that Downing is able to envision the skin he manipulates: to see the purpose of the mid-set jaw of the squirrel, to so accurately position the rolling *harmp* of the wolf's haunch, the split-beak *shock* of the long-tailed tit – but it is in Big Game that Downing truly shines, and right now the man (so pale! so anemic-looking!) is hovering over the skin of a grand Bengal tiger in the warm, well-lit back room of his taxidermy shop.

There are no chairs. Downing's workshop is no more

than ten meters wide, ten meters long, just enough to house two battered pine workbenches. A lone, quiet window illuminates a trio of shelves holding rows of fat glass bottles filled with beeswax, with mixed cedar oils, with salt of tartar, with palm wine, and they are next to chalky plasters and earth-and-water clays, any number of arsenical soaps and limes, astringents and powders, and though Downing can no longer smell it, for it has leaked into his skin, into his clothes, into what chestnut down remains of his hair, surrounding everything is *rosemary*: the omnipotent pine-sweet of camphor.

At the end of one workbench, next to a flat whetstone, wrapped in a fold of polished cow leather and twine, are the taxidermist's tools. For as the unskilled artisan surrounds himself with a great array of unnecessary items, those which he calls upon fruitlessly, the skilled artisan selects what he calls 'the fine few,' and these, for Downing, are: 1. a classic, indispensable skinning knife, the blade's cheek long, belly narrow, and bearing a handle made from a bright *lignum vitae*; 2. a broader model of the classic, indispensable skinning knife, with a larger belly, intended for heavier work; and 3. a saw-knife for the roughest work, the perforated blade with its wooden handle firmly attached to the plunge line with a polished brass ferrule.

Hanging from old nails on the wall are two dissecting scalpels procured from a London surgical instrument maker, two pairs of scissors (one to slice, one to prune), one pair of chunky bell hangers' pliers, and a large cloth pouch holding the piercing awl, the slender brainspoon, a pair of cutting nippers used chiefly by watchmakers, a straight stuffing iron (for this, Downing employs a bartender's old stirring spoon), and finally a hip-shaped pair of gentle tow forceps, when the work demands extraordinary prudence, and it is the tow forceps which Titus Downing grips now as he hovers over the skin of the grand Bengal tiger.

It was *truly* a very grand Bengal tiger, with fur the color of fire, and Downing has spent most of the past forty-eight hours bent-backed and lost in a dreamy, nighspiritual state, feeling tall grasses blow upon his gigantic wet nose, his heavy paws dropping on jungle floor, the ancient taste of blood in his mouth, and he nearly *owns* now the beast's natural pace, all its breath-pauses, and most importantly, its ceaseless, inviolable hunger, the motivation for its whole inviolable animus, when there's a knock on the door –

'Butter upon bacon!' the taxidermist exclaims, his eyeglasses slipping to the end of his nose.

He grabs what is left of the hair on his head and stomps to the front door of his shop, which opens with a jingle of sleigh bells.

'What *is* it!' he demands.

It is not a what but a who, a delivery boy, just skin and bones really, and with no mental capacity for taxidermy. The delivery boy, terrified of Mr Downing and his weird shop brimming with stuffed beasts, struggles to hold the very large brown paper package which he carries, corpse-like, in his arms.

'Sign for it, sir,' he says, and Downing, eyeing the package that has been marked *Karoo, Orycteropus afer*:

'*The Aardvark*' by the hand of his good friend Sir Richard Ostlet, Britain's finest zoological sportsman, signs for it.

He closes the door.

Downing carries the package back into his shop, holds it high in the light like an offering, and then returns to his back room and lays it gently down upon the unoccupied workbench. He unwraps the package and unfolds a death mask. Here, two rabbity ears. A rubber snout. The low mouth is shaped like a biscuit. Here, a thick and broad yellow-pink hide with four brown and furry hoof-claws. Here, an unassembled skeleton of blanched ribs and blanched feet, two fat bone-blades of shoulders, one long, pointed skull, and beneath it all a stack of accompanying notes and charcoal-sketches of a creature the likes of which no one in Warwickshire has ever seen.

∽

No one knows that you suck Greg Tampico's cock. And certainly no one knows that Greg Tampico sucks your cock, or that occasionally you will just lie in bed next to each other and stroke (or not stroke) each other's cocks.

You know that you are Not Gay, and Greg Tampico is Not Gay: you are simply both straight guys who occasionally like other straight guys who like to suck or stroke cocks – and no one yet knows that you met Greg Tampico eight months ago at a fundraising dinner for Namibian children with some horrible disfiguring disease that you had to promptly forget about, or even that Greg Tampico contacted you to come support his cause at the dinner a year ago because you were enjoying a 64% Favorability Rating then and were bringing with you, like, *seriously* great press!

No one saw how you gazed admiringly at each other across the ballroom, across the tables all adorned with English bone china, across the glittering chandeliers and candles as lukewarm chicken piccata and some kind of scampi were served, and no one could have noticed how quickly you discerned that the beautiful young woman in the seat next to yours was a complete idiot, or how you moved your seat a few inches back from hers to keep Greg Tampico, bright blond in his tuxedo, within your line of sight throughout dinner, after which you and Greg Tampico found yourselves in an alley off the kitchen (it was raining), leaning your backs against cold brick as he snapped a Zippo, or how you huddled together under the roofline, sharing a cigarette before making plans to go back to his place in Alexandria – *Alexander in Alexandria,* he said with a smile – or how you drove to his place on King Street, parked and made your way to his walk-up, where Greg Tampico was waiting to greet you, tie-loosened, in the foyer before he pulled you inside, led you upstairs, right into the bedroom and, laughing like a child at play, said, *Who's gonna be your lawyer, son,* as he reached for your belt buckle.

Using Representative Olioke's shitty rusted paring knife to saw down the sides of the cardboard box, which, when flat, creates a gigantic cardboard cross on the floor of your living room, you wonder why the *hell* Greg Tampico would send you his tremendous taxidermied aardvark, the stuffed creature which usually stands on an imitation Louis XIV French dresser parked directly across from his bed, watching as you handle Greg Tampico's cock or as Greg Tampico handles yours.

The aardvark, far as you know, is the only body of taxidermy owned by Greg Tampico, though in his walk-up he also displays assorted African masks, warthog tusks.

A collection of skulls from impala.

Greg Tampico has been to southern Africa many times for his foundation, and you do not worry about it when you cannot recall if Greg Tampico ever even *told you* where he goes in Namibia – in fact, whenever you lie naked on top of the man's authentic-zebra-pelt bedspread, his foundation is not even, like, *remotely* something you think about, and it is certainly not something you are thinking about as you tip the mounted aardvark over onto its side and discover an envelope.

It is a clean, vanilla-colored envelope, and when you open it, a piece of paper says, stamped in gold, FROM THE DESK OF GREGORY TAMPICO, PRESIDENT, THE HAPPINESS FOUNDATION and that is *all* it says. Beneath the heading, where a personal message should be, there is no personal message.

You are disconcerted. The entire thing – the aardvark, the blank note – is disconcerting to say the *least,* and you pick up your phone to call Greg Tampico and remember that nothing is working, but now suddenly everything's working. In the past five minutes, you have accrued 147 text messages and 48 emails, but this is standard. They are all from your staffers. None are from Tampico.

You scroll through your phone. You bring up his name. *aardvark?* you text.

∽

Titus Downing: consciously unmarried, consciously child-less, aficionado not only of taxidermy but also of very fine, very thin oxtail soup, gazes at the humped back and smooth neck, the fat claws, the ears and snout so oddly long it looks like someone pulled them, and shudders.

Next to the Bengal tiger, this so-called 'aardvark' is a truly vulgar creature, he thinks, ugly even for Nature, like a pig screwed a donkey, and immediately reminds Downing of a story famous among taxidermists, that of Captain John Hunter, who in 1798 sent the first skin and sketch of a platypus to naturalists in England who, in turn, assumed it was a hoax; they thought someone had sewn a duck's bill onto a beaver pelt, going so far as to write that 'upon Viewing the creature, it is impossible not to entertain doubts' and 'all surmise that there might have been practiced some art of deception,' which is why Downing, wondering if his close friend Richard Ostlet could have sent him a hoax, inspects the skin for unnatural seams and finds that there are no unnatural seams.

Downing returns to his workbench. He closes his eyes and tries to quiet himself back into the life of the Bengal tiger, but it is impossible, the tiger's moment has passed, it will likely take *days* to find it again, and his mind is traveling helplessly back to the aardvark until at last he gives up and goes to it, realizing with growing excitement that Ostlet has offered him not a joke but a *challenge*: how to re-create the *jiva* of a beast as ugly as this one? A creature about which no civilized man knows anything?

The notes and sketches which Ostlet has sent him now appear to Downing to be almost deliberately sparse:

> *Nocturnal. Sleeps in underground tunnels.*
> *Social, entomological eater. Has cheek teeth.*
> *Throws snout into ground to smell deeply.*
> *Digs with front feet. Kicks dirt with back feet.*
> *Bark is high pitched, such as a wanting dog.*

Exit the tiger, enter the aardvark. Downing's bony fingers cross the pelage. The skin is first pink and then yellow, the fur an inexplicable mixture of wire and silk, and it's brown at the hind limbs, which are plantigrade at the front, digitigrade at the back, and Ostlet's hunters always do a *very* fine job, he thinks as his hands touch the beast's rear feet, which take up half the leg. Then it's the heavy claws, each digit wide as a spoon, and what strength in the *tail*, Downing thinks, how it glides *right up the back*, which is round as a tortoise, and he closes his eyes and imagines the aardvark using the tail muscle for balance in her underground tunnels, to avoid bumping her wide body into narrow walls, and Downing can now clearly see the aardvark lumbering on her large legs past huge termite mounds – they look like sand castles built by ambitious, imbecilic children – and there's the great hulk of shoulder gliding beneath the skin, the fat swing of belly, and Downing now knows her weight and *pesanteur,* her erratic mood, and when she runs, she rises surprisingly up onto her tippy toes so much so she fairly *prances,* her conical head aloft with donkey ears that flick upward at any rustle of subterranean insect activity, and he can almost feel the scrabble of the loose soil as she thrusts her spoons into the earth to begin burrowing, the dirt smells of sugar, he can almost taste the nectar of termites now on his own sticky tongue until morning arrives and enter the bark, the soft piggy squeal: *don't wake me in daylight!*

Enter the fatigue, bones burning after a night ambling on these bizarre haunches, and when she sleeps, she curls her fat body into a comma, and Downing can feel the light purr of the beast's slimy lips during slumber, her nostrils shuttering open then closed, and there goes the slip of the serpentine tongue in and out from her small mouth as she dreams about her own hunger, and it is now, because Downing can see into the dreams of the ugly, vulgar, exhausted aardvark, that he begins to understand that despite its appalling morphology, *beauty is possible.*

❦

Greg Tampico does not text back. Greg Tampico always texts back. A chill creeps your neck as the stuffed aardvark, standing underneath a floor lamp, watches you pace in your living room. The way it's mounted, the front right claw slightly lifted, the long-snouted head slightly askew, ears alert, akimbo, the aardvark appears to be in the middle of walking to someplace important, like you have interrupted it *doing its job,* and the last thing you need right now is to feel you are, like, *bothering somebody in your own house,* but the creature's expression, while you never thought much about it in Greg Tampico's walk-up, here in your living room with your furniture precisely chosen to look like a townhouse Ronald Reagan might have enjoyed, is now looking, let's face it, like, *incredibly odd,* and you know that as soon as Congress is back in session and representatives Rutledge and Olioke are back in the townhouse, you will have to suffer their questions about the aardvark, and frankly?

You have no idea what in the hell you're going to tell them.

You go upstairs. You want to take a shower. Your shower is a Kohler Vibrant Brushed Bronze WaterTile Ambient Rain Overhead Rain Shower which cost $4125, so you like taking showers.

The water is cold. It feels good. It's so hot out.

You must be feeling this way from the heat, you think, and since Greg Tampico is not texting back, you decide while drying off with your $339 Hermès Sarcoline Terrycloth Body Towel that the easiest solution is to drive the aardvark to Alexandria and simply return it to him.

Motherof*god,* you think, what a pain in the *ass,* as you dress yourself, head to toe, in light casual summerwear from J. Crew.

When you return to the living room, the aardvark looks at you like you are ridiculous.

'Oh *no* you don't,' you say.

You have spoken out loud to a stuffed aardvark. You feel ridiculous.

You go into the kitchen and eat a few grapes.

While in the kitchen, which is floor-to-ceiling white subway tile decked out in $6000 worth of Williams-Sonoma that you never use, an epiphany: you open a cabinet. You remove a flour sack. It is a clean, white flour sack with a ragged edge to make it look vintage, and your decorator bought all these freaking flour sacks, instead of dishtowels, you have no idea why, but they're folded like new T-shirts in a cabinet in your kitchen, so you grab one and go back to the living room.

Though you feel stupid doing it, you cover the face of the aardvark with a flour sack.

Then, using your back and your knees like your old gym teacher taught you, you actually hoist the bastard, carrying it downstairs to the small, dark garage of 2486 Asher Place where your car, a black Chevy Tahoe, is waiting.

You leased the Tahoe just a few weeks ago for $600 monthly, and how pleased are you that the Tahoe is already proving itself useful as you fling open the rear doors and pull down the back seats. Remarkably, the aardvark fits. It's like the engineers planned it: THE TRUNK, LUXURIOUS AND ROOMY, CAN FIT A WHOLE AFRICAN AARDVARK!

You slam the doors, climb into the driver's seat and turn on the A/C and Soulja Boy, full blast. You hit the garage door button and the machine hums as the door rises.

The garage floods with sunlight.

You pull out onto the street, checking your phone. Though it is just 8:52 a.m., you now have 233 text messages and 97 emails, but this is, again, standard. You locate Greg Tampico's address on King Street in Alexandria, stab the GPS button, and are able to relax for the first time today as the Tahoe, worth every penny, knows what to do.

∽

Any piece of taxidermy begins with the mount, and for the aardvark, Titus Downing has chosen a thick piece of Leadwood the color of raisins, and it's a block of heavy wood which he has specially ordered from Namibia, and it took several weeks to get here, and it's finally here. The taxidermist spends whole days sawing and sanding the mount, which he then polishes, glossing it up with several coats of shellac, and when it is dry, he selects two iron rods: one straight, to stand upright and center, the other a convex curve to screw on top of the first, to support the aardvark's spine, neck to tail.

Together, the two rods look like a melting T, and when both are secured, the mount is now ready for what's called 'the mannequin.'

Downing builds every skin that arrives in his shop its very own mannequin, and the mannequin, made solely of wire and water clay, is a sloppy process demanding of its maker a great deal of patience and care. Downing measures the skin with the patience of a parent to decide how much clay will be required and today learns that the full length of the aardvark, at least this particular aardvark, tail to snout, over the hump, is an astonishing two-point-two meters, and the girth, the full circumference of belly and back, is an astonishing one-point-one meters, and Downing wonders if the aardvark wasn't more than just a *bit* on the fat side, which means that she was a good hunter. Which means that part of her *jiva* must be her *alertness,* her *good hearing,* and as he strokes the aardvark's silky ears, he studies the sketches provided by Ostlet to figure out whether the ears should stick up or hang down.

Ostlet's assistant has drawn them down.

Downing well knows that sketches alone cannot be trusted, that beasts before stuffing are often drawn after death, and, based on what he knows of the ears of Common Mammals, deduces from his Darwin that the long ears must *serve a purpose,* they must stick up to hear better, so after Downing builds the mannequin upon which the skin of the aardvark, padded with the finest wool from his father's farm in Northumberland, will hang, he affixes two wiry spires moving out from the base of the neck, and is ready.

Downing carefully lifts the aardvark's spine, drooping it over the curved rod of the mount. How the shoulder blades of the forearms *do* fan into paddles, he marvels, before they swoop back, dropping to the elbows, which reach amazingly under the rib cage before shooting straight down to the peroneus longus, the metatarsi, phalanges.

He hoists the hind legs – they are bulky, prodigious – and all at once the spine and the forelegs are positioned straight on the mount and the hind legs take their shape into a thick, splendid Z. How low the tailbone is, Downing observes as he wets both of his hands in a bucket. How like a dipped oar, *nearly touching* the two jaunty rear heels!

Although some taxidermists use only the leg bones and skull, slap-dashing the body and neck with odd cloths, with netting, burlap or sisal, which is then dipped into plaster, Downing uses everything that Ostlet has sent him, all the way down to the last wee bit of vertebra as there is less chance of an error this way, and he is, after twenty-five long years of practice, by now quite comfortable affixing the bones with water clay, and the water clay is sort of his favorite part, actually.

Titus Downing stares at the completed skeleton of the aardvark. He licks his lips, throws his dripping hands into the thick blocks of clay, and then the taxidermist begins his shaping.

∽

'Crank That' is blasting at top volume as you thumb through your now 389 unread text messages and 221 unread emails and head toward Alexandria via the George Washington Memorial Parkway, and you like taking the Parkway because it runs right past National – Reagan National – your favorite airport of all airports, with the most awesomesauce view of the Potomac, the Washington, Jefferson, and Lincoln monuments, and it is your favorite route because, while you take it, you enjoy imagining there one day being an Alexander Paine Wilson (R) monument.

Ronald Reagan's middle name was Wilson. You are not related. Nor are you related to Woodrow Wilson, a Democrat whose economic policies disgust you but whose international policies you admire (neo-imperialist Wilsonianism, now *that's* some shit you can get behind); but you are, as it happens, in a webby way, actually related to Thomas Paine, founding father, author of the famous 1776 Revolutionary doctrine *Common Sense,* and it is in the spirit of Thomas Paine that you have been working on your own missive for your reelection campaign.

The document, punned *Plaine Truth: Addressed to Reasonable Citizens of America,* is a combination of the original title of *Common Sense* and your middle name, and although none of your staffers is yet 100% behind *Plaine Truth,* you know that Fox will go crazy for it. Just like your relative Thomas Paine vigorously advocated for the separation of the colonies from Great Britain when he wrote, 'the weeping voice of Nature cries, 'TIS TIME TO PART,' you vigorously advocate for the separation of the United States, Democrats and Republicans. 'It's time for Two Americas,' you have written in *Plaine Truth,* ''TIS TIME TO PART,' and should this not, you explain to your staffers, be your rallying cry? Can't they, like, even *see* the bumper stickers?

DIVIDE TO UNITE
ALEXANDER PAINE WILSON 2020

When Greg Tampico read *Plaine Truth,* he got very choked up. He knew you were a Federalist, he said, and this idea was radical but it was also maybe kind of genius, he said, and wanted to know was there a map in the works? What would be the new borders?

And you murmured face-deep into his pillow: 'Details, details.'

It was no matter. *Plaine Truth,* Greg Tampico said, baby-kissing your Dimples of Apollo, was going to, like, *change the world* – and as you hurtle the Tahoe past the airport in your J. Crew, you're thinking *man,* how *gullible* Tampico is; how any dummy would know that you only like *Plaine Truth* because the position is freaking *tested,* the Red States are ready to split, it freaking *guarantees an electorate,* and no politician worth his, you know, *salt* or whatever would ever support anything without the guarantee of his electorate, and while thinking about this you catch a glimpse of yourself in the rearview, and how *seriously great* are you looking in your vintage '80s Ray-Bans, the same pair you've had since the early Aughts at UVA?

You start talking out loud. 'Alexander Paine Wilson National Airport,' you say, and, 'Wilson National,' alternately glancing at the Ray-Bans and scrolling through emails, when a subject heading catches your eye that warrants your complete and total attention:

Tampico dead.

∽

Whereas for the giraffe, Downing portioned off the water clay mould into separate sections, building the mannequin piece by piece in his workshop, for the aardvark, the taxidermist creates one single contiguous mould, pulling his hands toward his chest as he strokes, and the man's thin fingers are surprisingly strong, moving skillfully over the paddles, the perfect ovum of rib cage, following no other plan than the map of his own instinct, all the way to the rear oar at which point Downing steps back, studies what he has done, and readies himself for what is always the most difficult work: the death mask.

The *jiva*, Downing knows, life's immortal essence, it lives in the face. Within the face, it lives in the eyes. They must be just right. If the eyes are not just right, the animal will look at best like a joke, at worst like a nightmare, so for the aardvark's eyes, Titus Downing spends hours selecting from a vast assortment of beads. The beads, painted and wooden, too large or too small, do not work on the aardvark.

The dead thing just somehow looks deader.

The snout, Downing observes, annoyed, is also off: though malleable, it sticks out *straight,* and that's when he realizes that the position of the whole head is wrong. It's too high. He's been building the entire front half of the aardvark *too high,* and the hump of the beast's back tells him that it wouldn't walk with its head raised up like that, and so Downing has to start over. Destroy everything.

It's not the first time this has happened. It won't be the last.

Though it creates a terrific, wet mess, with requisite patience, Downing washes the clay off the skeleton. He repositions all netting and wire. He removes the long, curved rod, the hat of the T, and replaces it with a shorter one, to lower the neck joints. He reassembles the wires and once again wets his hands, thrusts them into clay, and when the mannequin is fully rebuilt, he tilts the wires which reposition the ears, and when he hangs the carcass now? *There* she is, alert and listening, giving Downing a *slight sideways glance* as though Downing is interrupting her at her night-work, and at once the aardvark looks neither special nor strange but quotidian.

He lifts the front right hoof forward, casually displaying one black-footed claw. She is walking.

For a moment, Downing is pleased – with all but the eyes. The beads *still* do not look right, and over the next few days, Downing tries every kind and size of bead he owns, but nothing is working, and the more time he spends staring at the face of the aardvark, the more restless he feels. Trying to correctly visualize the aardvark's expression with her long lashes, her coarse whiskers launching ludicrously outward from under the eyelids like two misplaced mustaches, is now keeping him awake nights, and since Downing works alone and is unmarried and without children, no one notices or cares for him, and so it goes until, early one afternoon, he catches himself swooning at his workbench. He nearly faints. He must stop, he must eat something.

And what he eats must be nourishing.

With a happy jingle of sleigh bells, Titus Downing leaves his taxidermy shop and walks outside, underneath the twelve stag heads. It is a hot blue British day, all noise and summer, yet Downing, who wears the same black woolen suit every month of the year, hardly notices, for there are no seasons for an artist. Though he can hear the horses clopping down Victoria Terrace, tossing their glossy heads, ringing their neck bells, though he can see finely dressed couples enter and exit Jephson Gardens, promenading the River Leam for exercise, for fresh air, the taxidermist does not take one single cognizant breath. He feels certain that taking a deep breath of anything will kill him outright, and proceeds quickly past the old Royal Pump Rooms with their purported healing waters, which made Leamington Spa famous a few decades past (but turned out to be, the townsfolk learned, quite polluted), and Titus Downing crosses the graveled paths of the new Pump Room Gardens, skirts darkly down Bedford Street, around the corner to the once-bustling-but-now-nearly-vacant Regent Street, to the butcher's where he buys himself the lone tail of an ox to make oxtail soup.

The exchange happens in silence.

The butcher does not speak when Downing enters.

Others in the shop, too, when they see Downing's wan, glowering face enter, quietly watch him collect his small parcel as though it's the first time they have ever set eyes on the man (for many, it must be said, that may well be), and none of this bothers Titus Downing in the slightest. He has never enjoyed sharing pleasantries over the exchange of goods and services; the taxidermist, over the years, has learned that he has little use for people in general, but finds himself surprised, slightly touched, when he returns home and opens the package in his small kitchen and discovers that the butcher – perhaps noticing how very thin Downing looks, how very pale, even in the sweltering endboil of summer – has gifted him with not just the tail but a large eye from the ox as well.

The eye is glassy, glorious, with a rainbow-colored iris which is positively *glowing*, and it is then that Downing, in a near-delirium born out of hunger, exhaustion, sees that what taxidermists have done this past century is all wrong! Darwin and Edmonstone and all of them for years used painted beads for the eyes of any beast not killed on local terrain – eyes rot during transport – but how could anyone properly capture the *jiva* using *beads*?

After all, Downing thinks, wood is *dead*, too-homogenous, and paint, it is wanting, and he needs to re-create nuanced colors of the eyes of the aardvark, the iris and sclera, and he can do it with *glass*.

There is one glassmith Downing knows in Leamington Spa. But he only blows fruit bowls. Glass cups and glass vases. The only man in the world Downing knows who can make him a set of glass eyes must be Harold Skinner, Downing's former roommate at Oxford, now a respected prosthetic specialist in London who used to make dolls' eyes and now makes human eyes, replicas for soldiers, blind people, and so, Downing decides, it means a trip to London.

London has been on Downing's brain as of late, but only in the way the promise of excitement haunts an artist who finds himself buried in the tedium of making. London was a notion planted early in the week when Downing received a card in the mail, an invitation from Lady Rebecca Ostlet, Richard Ostlet's new wife, the young botanist, to visit her, an invitation Downing had deliberately planned to ignore but now deliberately plans to accept, as it must mean that Richard has returned from Africa, and Downing, now armed with a reason, can suddenly see the two of them together journeying to Harold Skinner to order the glass eyes and then going for pints at a public house Richard enjoys, Ye Olde Mitre in Farringdon, where Ostlet (round and jolly) and Downing (thin and dour) will sit side by side at a small table in a corner for hours with their feet flat on the red carpet, their backs slumped against the dark wood (it is summer; there won't be a fire), discussing the aardvark until they go red-faced and sweaty, relaxing from drink, and Downing can now so easily *picture* how the whole thing will play out from there.

Setting himself to write to Rebecca Ostlet, Downing does not worry about the fact that his friend Richard has married, nor that he, Downing, was not invited to the wedding, nor even, particularly, that the invitation has come from the wife and not the man himself. Rebecca Ostlet would like to see him on 'rather pressing business,' she has written, requesting a hasty 'Return of Post,' and would Titus Downing accept an invitation to stay with her at the Ostlet household, now conveniently located in Kensington, on Gloucester Walk, a mere hour from the British Museum – which, as it happens, is displaying the excavated remains of the Temple of Artemis at Ephesus, an exhibit she feels he might enjoy Viewing?

So given that Downing believes he is at a point where he might safely break from his work without losing his sense of the aardvark's *jiva*, given that he urgently needs to contact Skinner, given his longing to see Richard, his closest friend, Downing accepts the invitation, conveying to Lady Ostlet that she might expect him to arrive at their doorstep in two days, specifically, this Friday teatime.

～

The email is from a staffer. It was delivered to your inbox last night at 2:08 a.m., when you were asleep, was waiting at the very bottom of your unread messages, which is why you are only seeing it now. You tap it and read the short news brief, which reports that Mr Gregory Tampico, president of the Happiness Foundation, an organization offering medical assistance to Namibian children, committed suicide two days ago in his apartment in Alexandria.

The funeral, it says, is tomorrow, two o'clock, at Murphy & Milliken's Funeral Home on Prince Street.

The news shocks you. But there is a part of you that is also relieved. Like, *of course it is terrible* when anyone takes his own life, like, *you're no monster*, but now there's zero possibility that anyone will ever find out about you and Greg Tampico, and, let's face it, that was some fairly unsavory business you got yourself mixed up in, and it all could have gotten worse, much, *much* worse – so yes, you do feel shock, relief, but there is also some guilt: for you now recall how Greg Tampico had asked you only two weeks ago if he might come work for you, how he could not stand seeing you just once a month *if that*, and wouldn't you both have a great time traveling the country, he said, campaigning together, and he had already arranged for a kick-ass parasailing trip off the Oregon coast because he knew how much you like parasailing.

He could help you, he said, you know, *relax on the trail*, and you could even go hiking and camping and other wildernessy stuff, and he had this idea for promoting *Plaine Truth* involving divvying up and privatizing the national parks. You could be an updated, inverse Roosevelt, he explained, outfitted with a lodge in, like, *Montana or something*, and you could even pick up hunting as you led your half of America – Right America – by capitalizing on her natural wildernesses ('The Grand Canyon, brought to you by Tampax,' he laughed), and how *great* would you look in the publicity pictures hiking one of the minor mountain ranges decked out in North Face, Patagonia –

'Okay, *Brokeback*,' you said.

'I don't mean like *that*,' he said.

'What about the foundation,' you said.

'What about it,' he said.

'Don't you have that responsibility,' you said.

Greg Tampico said that he'd just given notice at the foundation. He'd been at his job for twelve years. He felt he'd done good. He'd helped many, many children in Namibia, he said, and believed the time had come to step down. Besides, he'd been feeling blue lately, he confessed, and knew he could be a great asset as one of your staffers – or maybe even your director of communications or something – but as Tampico said what he was thinking, you were thinking, *Of course this changes everything*.

You had to apologize. Told Greg Tampico that something came up and climbed out of his bed. You began dressing yourself, in front of the aardvark. You had to go, you said, and he looked pretty crestfallen.

He asked when he was going to see you next.

You shrugged. You didn't know, you said, but it could be a while given that you were going to be doing your regular governing work along with your reelection campaign, and that's when Greg Tampico had actually started to fucking *cry*, and suddenly the walk-up in Alexandria with all his weird African masks and African prints and the gigantic stuffed aardvark that was always looking at you with the oddest expression?

It creeped you right out.

You would call him, you said, maybe next week, and did not look at his face as you walked out the door because you could not have gotten out of there fast enough.

So you could not have known how Greg Tampico collapsed on his bed. Or how hard he sobbed when he heard you sprint all the way down the three flights of stairs, knowing, at that moment, that he would never see you again, and that's why as the news sinks in you feel *bad* about it, but mostly you feel lighter, unencumbered, if truth be told, and you're even breathing differently now, like the news moved the lungs in your chest.

You signal the Tahoe and make a uwee toward home. Because the fact is, you rarely think about Greg Tampico at all when you are out of that apartment, and you are now growing just, like, *incredibly* relieved that you never brought him to 2486 Asher Place. It means Greg Tampico never saw your canary-yellow velvet Victorian sofa just like the one Reagan had in *Images of Greatness,* or your growing wardrobe of clothes just like Reagan wore. Or Reagan's original American flag cuff links, which you bought at an auction for a whopping $5900 and break out just for debates.

He never knew that you once even put in a bid to buy a vial of Reagan's blood from when Hinckley shot him, nor that your anonymous bid was in the tens of thousands before news of the auction was leaked to the media and shut down from 'poor taste,' and you assure yourself that, in general, you cannot feel all that bad about Greg Tampico's suicide because Greg Tampico never *really* knew you, never knew the full depth of your ambition, the lengths to which you know you will have to go to get reelected, to start getting serious, which is why upon hearing the news about Greg Tampico, you decide your staffers are right. It's time to get serious.

It's time for Congressman Alexander Paine Wilson to Find A Wife.

∽

Enter Kensington, an elegant, leafy borough in the west of London, neighbour to Chelsea. Enter the excellent road Gloucester Walk, nestled between two verdant parks, Holland and Hyde. Enter Rebecca Ostlet's modest two-bedroom flat, which suits her because the parks are where Rebecca goes walking in the afternoons with her three rust-colored Irish setters named after the Brontës – Anne, Charlotte, Emily.

'Come in, come in!' begs Rebecca, and Titus Downing,

dressed head to toe in his black wool even though it is a brutally hot day in August, steps into Rebecca's abode exactly like a ghoul into a garden.

The flat, furnished with an army of upholstered pink chairs, upholstered pink settees and sofas, ornate gilded frames and vases from the Orient, is wallpapered, floor to ceiling, in decorous pink roses, and there is a painted secretaire in one corner also covered in roses, and the curtains, too, are rose-pink, and her floors have been recently polished with rose-petal oil, and flowers of every rose breed hang their heads in her windows, and the dogs, just bathed and clipped, even smell rosy.

When Lady Ostlet asks Downing to make himself comfortable, to take a seat, the man, accustomed to the scent of earthy animal skins, of chloroforms, formaldehydes, oxides and an occasional tobacco product of some kind, glances around the place and is acutely perplexed: there are too many places to sit, for one; for two, every place is right next to some fecund belly of flowers; and for three, Downing also knows that once he sits, the Brontës will be instantly upon him.

He must linger too long in deciding because Rebecca grabs him by the arm and says, 'Please, first let me show you your room,' and leads him to the room where he will be staying for two what appear to be absolutely *interminable* days, and he considers bowing out of the whole thing entirely until Rebecca opens the door and he finds the walls of the guest room at the Ostlets' city flat to be dark green and *sans fleurs*.

There is a 17th-century wooden writing desk with the

requisite paper and inkwell. A single bed with brass knobs in the shape of pheasant heads. On top of the bed, a folded white coverlet, nothing more.

An ashtray is perched thoughtfully upon a small table by the window next to an assortment of books, titles from which Downing, whose thoughts remain with the aardvark, can deduce no hidden meaning: *Man and Wife,* by Wilkie Collins, Trollope's latest, *Phineas Redux,* and a faded copy of Jane Austen's *Persuasion.* He notices only the absence of any Dickens and Dickens is his favorite.

'It's perfect, thank you,' says Downing.

'Oh *good,*' says Rebecca Ostlet, and claps her hands, escorting Downing back into the parlor where a tea setting of scones with jam and clotted cream have magically appeared.

After Downing eats and drinks he relaxes some, but he is always uncomfortable in the company of women. He wishes today were tomorrow. He has scheduled an appointment with Skinner tomorrow and knows that the aardvark, once completed, is going to be even more thrilling than the giraffe, so as Downing speaks perfunctorily with Lady Ostlet, he loses himself in a dream of crowds coming out in gaggles to View it.

Women, he has heard, upon seeing strange animals have been known to faint, and Downing allows himself to imagine that perhaps it will be the story of the fainting women that will make the aardvark extremely valuable, eventually purchased by the New Walk for a very high price, and this, combined with the success of the giraffe, will enable him to pay off the remaining balance on his shop, easing him into retirement or, if he allows himself to dream as deeply as he only rarely dares to dream, a bit of travel – and so it is that Downing only *purports* to appear interested in Rebecca Ostlet as she chats with him about his life in Leamington Spa, but he is obviously uninterested until, after some minutes pass, he notices that the woman, a brunette dressed in simple black crêpe, the collar and cuffs edged in black piping, well-aged at twenty-eight, pretty/plain in the manner of the era (though perhaps a bit *too* narrow chested), is nervous. Her hands quiver unsteadily when she drinks her tea. Her small eyes seem to dart around the room as though of their own will.

Lady Ostlet is constantly looking out of the window, Downing realizes, and it is not long before it becomes obvious that the woman is eager to get to the matter at hand, and the matter at hand is, of course, the absence of her husband, Sir Richard.

Downing is polite. He waits for a pause in the conversation before clearing his throat. He asks delicately, with care, but not so much care as to appear probing:

'Where is your husband?'

Rebecca Ostlet lowers her head and stares through the rose bundles tipping neatly in the Oriental vases stationed in her front windows. She is gazing forlornly at the brick side of Gloucester Walk, and Downing now worries: while he is donning his usual gloomy black, the short frock coat which has long been his preference, he also displays on his person the smooth front of a white linen shirt, a textured brown brocade for a waistcoat, matching

Windsor scarf, and when he arrived at the flat, he removed his round, gray-ribboned Gambler, his beaver-skin gloves – but there is nothing on Rebecca Ostlet that is not black, and women, they wear full black only in mourning, and so something must have *happened* to his close friend, he coldly deduces, and this, whatever has *happened,* is the reason why Lady Ostlet has invited him to London, to share some kind of *bad news,* and if it is true, Downing wishes she could have just *written it, for the love of Christ,* for what's the point in receiving bad news in person when people like to grieve *in private,* and he barely *knows* this woman, and if the news is as bad as he thinks, it will be downright *rotten* for him because Rebecca Ostlet cannot know how close he and Richard were; how they had been first acquainted in a custodial closet at the Great Exhibition nearly a quarter century past when Downing was sixteen, Ostlet twenty-five, forging a fast friendship over their mutual interest in naturalism: Ostlet, an academic on the side of Mammalian Behavior, and Downing, a budding artist on the side of the Study and Preservation of Species – and there is even a small part of Downing that had imagined retiring somewhere close to Ostlet when the time came.

But then Sir Richard Ostlet went and married Rebecca Green, a woman half his age. He was talking about having children. As Downing was eagerly anticipating even quieter years ahead, Ostlet was eagerly anticipating some kind of comic recreation of a youth he never had, and what man at the age of *fifty,* Downing is thinking, would want to have a *child,* when the slim botanist at long last looks away from her windows, turns toward him and asks with shocking directness:

'Mr Downing, do you believe in life after death?'

∽

The Parkway, it is empty as you are scrolling your phone for the number of Tabitha Castle, daughter of the one and only Brian Castle, tech billionaire, and she is a tough, cheeky girl you have dated in the past who goes by, adorably, 'Toby.' Toby Castle is turning twenty-nine this year and you are turning thirty-five this year, and you and Toby always have a good enough time together, and you like seeing Toby, so you are going to pursue Toby.

Toby Castle is fit. Toby Castle is blond.

Toby Castle wears starched sleeveless dresses to show off her toned arms and directs a financial company that helps minor investment businesses get off the ground, and though it's all her father's tech money portioned off, investments in exchange for a whopping 85% return, 'Castle' is one of those names in Washington – hell, in America – and suddenly it's so easy to see you and Toby Castle hitting the social circuit, going to the fundraisers, the galas and balls, and you can, like, *definitely see yourself marrying Toby Castle,* living with Toby Castle in the townhouse, maybe starting a family (you have tasted her vagina, it's not terrible), and then, once you start a family, you won't have to live with Toby Castle anymore. You can do what representatives Rutledge and Olioke do, which is keep the family *outside of DC,* and it's how you'd prefer it since the truth of the matter is, it's nothing against women, but by and large they make you uncomfortable.

It's not about sex. It's like: women make you feel like a man, but men make you feel like a *human*. It's not your fault you are who you are, and they are who they are. After all, there are certain *biological facts* at work here, there is such a thing as Natural Law, and sure, we can call them Divine Principles if we have to appease evangelicals (secretly you do not believe in God, though you do, at times, atmospherically fear him), and you make a mental note to work on this idea about biology and theology for *Plaine Truth*.

Because it's not just women. There are also many minorities out there that make you uneasy, like black people or LGBT or whatever, but you do not take them seriously. LGBT sounds like something you'd order in a diner with mayo. As for black people, they only make up 13.4% of the population. Latinos are more.

You honestly have no problem with black people at all.

Representative Olioke is black, and even though you kind of hate Olioke, he is a Republican and you have always been friendly with him and he has always been friendly with you, and there is a part of you that's imagined, you admit, one day, like, *milking Olioke's blackness* by asking him to be your running mate.

'Divide to unite,' you imagine yourself saying in front of a huge crowd on the steps of the Capitol, and lose yourself for a second – okay, wait for it, *there* you are – standing in front of the white pillars on the bright white steps with five military planes overhead farting out clouds of red, white, and blue while you gently pull out your cuffs, fingering Reagan's flag cuff links, looking, like, *so fucking good* in that $4560 Calvin Klein mod-breasted silk suit.

And you neither now nor will ever recall the numerous parent–teacher conferences endured by your mother, nor the way she looked at you fearfully after the counselors said you were 'empathically . . . deficient.' *What does* that *mean,* you overheard her asking your father that evening, and he answered, *He's a jerk, that's what it means,* and your mother, she sighed. *Ever since he was born, I felt it,* she said, like they lived on the frontier, *felt it deep in ma bones,* and from that point on you extricated yourself from the both of them and do not care or even wonder what your parents will think when you are standing on the Capitol steps in the manner which you will most certainly one day be standing, waving to the teeming crowd, Olioke on your left, Toby Castle your right, embracing your waist, grinning, her adoration for you *positively unbridled,* and Brian Castle, one of the most famous billionaires in America, he is there too, he's behind you, proud father-in-law, wallet at the ready, and you really don't know why you even waited so long to call Toby Castle.

You find her name. You tap the screen.

When she answers, Toby does not say hello, she says: 'Hi, Asshole,' and you forgot how much you like that, and her voice sounds damned *terrific* if you want to be honest about it, and you immediately apologize for not calling her sooner.

Yes, you know it's been months, you say, and make a plan to meet that evening for dinner at that restaurant in Georgetown, she knows the one, with the name that sounds like a law office, where they only serve food in vintage tin lunchboxes and you have to recite a poem to get a menu.

The Brown, Lake & Peterson Company.

It's the last place you two went together, and even though you hate that hipster shit, you know girls love that hipster shit, and Toby wants to go there, and so when you decide to go there, she sounds tickled about it but also confident, like *she knows what you're up to* because, let's face it, you have mutual acquaintances, and your mutual acquaintances have already let Toby Castle in on the game: your staffers are pushing you to Find A Wife, she knows it all, and she was probably already expecting your call, but still – Toby sounds glad to hear from you, and that makes you glad, pretty glad, and when you end the call you are feeling great actually, just great, and you have forgotten all about Greg Tampico and the aardvark until you're about to cross the 14th Street Bridge and have to pull your Tahoe over to the side of the Parkway, because a cop, lights circling, has driven up right behind you.

∽

What a question to ask a *taxidermist*, thinks Downing as he stares at Rebecca Ostlet, and the question only sets him thinking further about the aardvark's *jiva*, about Darwin and the Guianese slave, about his belief that in order to truly succeed at the art of taxidermy one must supplicate before the animal, one must immerse one's soul into the creature's soul so that it, through Downing, may be reborn – and so the answer to Lady Ostlet's question is, to him, both blindingly simple and blindingly complex.

Downing settles his teacup and saucer deep in his palms. 'I do believe in life after death,' he says, and for this answer, Rebecca Ostlet looks relieved.

'Of all of Richard's friends,' she says, 'I knew that *you* would be the one to contact,' and proceeds to explain about her husband's strange, sudden death, about how she waited for weeks with no word until at last word arrived, and the word was terrible: about the pills of camphor he swallowed. About how he would never return from safari.

That Rebecca cannot make sense of the suicide, there is no doubt, but Downing guesses there is something more the woman wishes to ask of him, and the grisly thought does cross his mind that the woman has somehow *preserved the body* and is perversely hoping he might attempt to *stuff Richard,* but these ghastly concerns are allayed when Rebecca talks freely about the burial, about how they managed to secure a lot for the coffin in one of the cemeteries, in Kensal Green – a relief, she says, given the lack of space in the churchyards – and as she says this, Rebecca shudders in a very conventional, female way, and if Downing were another man, he would go and put his arm around her, but at this moment he can only think about the utter impossibility of Ostlet, at least the Ostlet he knew, taking his own life.

'That's not possible,' he says.

'I *know,*' says Rebecca, and the Brontës, sensing her unhappiness, begin to circle her chair.

Titus Downing notices how dark the woman's eyes look. They are slightly swollen, and he can all at once observe the many nights Rebecca has stayed awake, weeping, but she is no longer weeping. She looks, if he can gauge it right, a little bit frightened.

'Titus,' Rebecca says, and finally shares with him the reason why she has called him to London:

After they buried him – just weeks ago, Lady Ostlet says – she saw her husband in his Wellington boots shuffling past their flat on Gloucester Walk.

'It's happened four times now,' she says.

These *women*, Downing swears, my god, they have *pudding* for brains, and even having to think about women having pudding for brains makes Downing feel dumber, and he truly does hate talking to women, and there must be *legions* of widows who have gone crazy in bereavement, believing they see their dead husbands everywhere, and Lady Ostlet's black dress and dark eyes and her three feathery dogs, her flat full of flowers, it all suddenly feels downright *insane,* but as he thinks this, he also must admit to himself that Rebecca Ostlet is not *acting* insane: her expression, though slightly fearful, is not panicked; in fact, she appears more curious than anything, and when she says '*Titus,*' in the intimate way that she does, placing her hand on the crook of his arm, and continues, 'he's *out there,*' and points at her street, it's the way she says 'out there' that sends a shudder through Titus Downing.

Rebecca Ostlet gives each of the Brontës a biscuit. 'But that's not the worst part,' she says.

'What's the worst part,' Downing says.

'When he walks by,' Rebecca says, 'there are bandages over his eyes.'

'Bandages why,' says Downing, because what can one possibly say to such a thing?

With both palms, Rebecca Ostlet smooths the middle parting in her hair. 'Because his eyes are not in his head.'

One of the Brontës jumps up onto Downing's lap and breathes on him. The dog's breath is warm, and Downing smells the sour contents of its stomach as Rebecca Ostlet stands up and walks to her secretaire.

It is a woman's secretaire, painted white with red roses, and it, to Downing, looks like a large toy as he watches Rebecca unlock and lower the lid. She produces a wooden specimen box, which Downing instantly recognizes as the same five-drawer specimen box which belonged to Richard. He watches as Rebecca pulls out one drawer of the box with two fingers, walks over to him until she is standing right in front of Downing and there, on the cork-lined bottom, is a small, fluid-filled, glass-lidded jar in which the isolated double oculi of Richard Ostlet are thickly floating.

৩

Cops are easy. All you have to do is show him your ID, explain you're a congressman. There will be some perfunctory chit-chat, and you will make the officer feel important, for you know, like, *providing the civil service that he provides,* and he may or may not write you a light traffic ticket or something, which is no problem – there is no problem that your staffers can't handle – and sure enough, when the officer approaches your Tahoe, asks for your license, registration, insurance, and you hand it over, all is going as it should go, and the officer is, like you, a young handsome white guy, and he even actually, like, *looks* a little bit like you, and you have no reason to imagine that anything will go wrong in the way that it's about to go wrong until he puts both hands over the side of your door and asks you what the hell you were doing all this time on your phone.

You grin. You apologize. O you *definitely* know better, you sing, but you are, after all, in the middle of a reelection campaign, the officer *must* understand, and you are heading back home right now to tend to the numerous things that need tending, and show him your ID again.

This, for some reason, makes him angry.

'I need to see your phone, Congressman,' he says, and sticks out his hand.

You give it to him and become slightly nervous watching the officer scroll through your phone like that, especially when he begins telling you that there are *new laws in place* for Distracted Driving, and he's been observing you ever since you made that illegal uwee, and he saw how you did not put down your phone *once* in ten whole minutes, and he even says it like that, like he's a toddler exaggerating some tiny injustice: *ten whole minutes*.

'Frankly, Congressman,' he says, 'I don't care who you are. If you're out here driving so recklessly, you're putting the public in danger.'

You affirm his position. Gosh, you tell him, he is *one*

hundred percent right. You should absolutely *not* be on your phone while driving, and you are grateful to him for helping you understand the new laws (even though you do feel they are stupid laws), and if he needs to write you a ticket you will understand.

From him, there is silence.

You ask him how the Boys on the Force are doing. If there's anything the Boys on the Force need that they're not getting from Congress, and you again gently remind him that you are a congressman and show him your ID at which point he glances at you, incredulous. He laughs out loud, and this laughing, it's now telling you that this officer is not on your side, he's not one of you, he's probably a fucking Democrat and there is no talking to Democrats, and so from that point on, you shut your mouth and let the officer do the talking, which, as it turns out, is a good idea because you are about to feel more than mildly impugned when the officer starts to unload on you about his wife, how she needed an emergency abortion to save her life and how you, Representative Alexander Paine Wilson (R), were one of the congressmen who voted in favor of Virginia's recently failed bill to ban all abortions after six weeks, who would have just let his wife *die* under the pretense of 'protecting life,' and that is why this officer – the name on his badge says ANDERSON – who lives in a shitty condo in Falls Church or someplace, is not only about to vote for Nancy Fucking Beavers, he is about to make the life of her opponent all kinds of gigantic living hell.

'Sir, step out of the vehicle,' Officer Anderson says.

You step out. The cop actually asks you to turn

around, and he's going to give you 'a pat down, okay?' he says, and so you find yourself red-faced and furious as you turn around on this brutally hot morning and place your hands on the brutally hot hood of the Tahoe as cars and trucks hurtle past, headed onto the bridge and right toward the Jefferson Memorial.

The officer's lights are circling. Everything smells like burnt rubber and oil, and you pray no one recognizes you as Officer Anderson slaps his hands up your legs, into your groin, and you are in the midst of deciding that you are going to report him to your staffers, they will take care of this, you know, no sweat, when he tells you to go to the back of the Tahoe and open it.

You walk to the back as a long row of freighter trucks screams past. The heat of the pavement hits you, the oil, the gas, it makes you light-headed, and you are thinking only about what world of shit this dickbag Officer Anderson is going to find himself in when he's done with you, which means you are not thinking at all about the cargo which you are carrying in the back of the Tahoe when you open the doors.

The police officer jumps back. 'What the hell is that!' he shouts.

Enter the aardvark, alight on its mount. Enter the aardvark, claw raised, head covered with a goddamned gourmet $22 dish towel that suddenly looks incredibly suspicious hanging over the head of an aardvark, like it's an infidel.

'It's an *aardvark*,' you say, and the officer yanks the flour sack off the aardvark's head like it will bite him, and yes, a gigantic taxidermied aardvark is taking up the trunk of your Tahoe.

Officer Anderson looks at you. 'What are you doing with a stuffed aardvark, Congressman.'

'I'm not doing anything with it,' you say.

'What's it for?'

You look like you don't understand what he is asking because you honestly don't understand what he's asking.

'Where's the permit,' he says.

'The what?'

'The *permit*. You need a federal permit to possess this wildlife,' he says.

You calmly explain that 'this wildlife' was delivered to your house just this morning. And if Officer Anderson wants, he can follow you back to Asher Place and you can show him the box, the big-ass cardboard box it was delivered in, but Anderson shakes his head. 'A federal taxidermy permit allows you to temporarily possess another's legally acquired wildlife,' he says, obvi rote from some book. 'It is unlawful for any person to import, export, transport, sell, receive, acquire, or purchase in interstate or foreign commerce any wildlife taken, possessed, transported, or sold in violation of any state or foreign law. It's called the "Lacey Act."'

Now you're mad. You *know* the goddamned Lacey Act, you say. But you didn't *steal it*, and you certainly didn't stuff it; it was, like, *given to you,* for Chrissakes! *It's a goddamned gift,* you insist, and you don't even realize the trap you've laid for yourself until it's too late.

Anderson looks at you sideways. 'All right,

Congressman,' he says, 'who *gave you* this aardvark? Whoever gave it to you should have given you the permit,' he says, and that's when you start imagining scenarios: like pushing Officer Anderson to the ground and jumping back into the Tahoe and speeding off; or like telling Officer Anderson to *Hey, wow, look at that weird bird in the sky,* and then punching Officer Anderson in his jaw and his gut and then jumping back in the Tahoe; or like, maybe, outsprinting Anderson on foot down the 14th Street Bridge, jumping over one side into the Potomac, swimming to shore, abandoning the Tahoe and aardvark and then somehow hailing an Uber; or just like *going for it* and grabbing Anderson's gun from his holster and turning yourself over to fate – but none of these are viable options in the 21st century. In the 21st century, cameras are everywhere. They are in Officer Anderson's cop car. They are on his body. They are recording you right now as you are hesitating to answer his question, and you can feel things getting bad, Anderson is getting suspicious, and so you resign yourself to the fourth option, the glorious refuge of rich young white men everywhere: pleading dumb.

The delivery box wasn't marked with a return address, you tell Anderson. Someone, you don't know who, sent this aardvark to you, you have no idea why, and seriously, people send congressmen, like, *super bizarre gifts all the time,* you say, which sends you into a long and clumsy story about Representative Rutledge once receiving a rabbit's foot on a chain from a constituent, and you can't really see the difference between something like this and a rabbit's foot.

Officer Anderson, alas, does not buy it.

'There's a *world of difference* between one rabbit's foot and an *entire aardvark*,' he says, clearly not believing you about the return address. 'The U.S. Postal Service will not deliver something without a return address,' he says, and that's when, with considerable relief, you remember the FedEx man with his bushy beard and his funny thick eyeglasses!

You fold your arms. You condescend to Anderson that it wasn't the *post office*; it was actually FedEx.

At which point the policeman visibly brightens.

'Great, I see,' he says. 'So all we need to do is get the tracking number,' and that's when you realize that, for now, he's got you. That if you follow through with your story, he's going to figure out the aardvark came from Greg Tampico, and your next move must be, can *only* be, to distance yourself from Greg Tampico as much as possible, and from here on out, Tampico's *a complete and total stranger*, because who, after all, knew about you and Greg Tampico other than you and Tampico?

Anderson asks you again for your phone, on which you now have 603 unread text messages and 410 unread emails. 'I think we better go down to the station,' he says, and begins to read you your Miranda.

2

THE HUMAN EYEBALL, DOWNING knows from his Darwin, contained in its cavity, was at first nothing but a light-sensitive patch. Some spot on some skin of some early creature, and the spot, made of nothing but nerve fibers and photoreceptors, all opsin and chromophore, gave these early creatures some survival advantage, for better or worse, a *sense of direction* until out from this blindness one day the spot deepened, creating an oculus, so let's widen the opening, create a space through which more light may enter, create a *fluid-filled chamber* wholly embraced by the photoreceptors so that the retina may enter, replete with a fine layer of pigment and cells until: enter the cornea, covering the chamber in the thinnest possible membrane until the membrane thickens, and the chamber fluid thickens into a *transparent humor*, at the front of which enters the lens. The cornea separates. The humor goes vitreous while retaining a separate aqueous chamber, to protect the iris, and it happens in a manner that enables the most expansive range of sight for what has come alive in the cavity, agented by new muscles, directed by nerves, and all is protected by the necessary appendages, the lids and brows, until what was once a very simple receptor able only to discern lightness and darkness, the daily synchronization of circadian rhythms, the human eyeball, round, white and semisolid, now becomes complex as a camera.

As Titus Downing looks at his close friend Sir Richard Ostlet's eyeballs floating preserved in the glass jar, he knows all of this to be true, yet there is no science that can explain how the eyeballs were taken out of Richard's head, how they came to arrive inside his specimen box along with other scant personal items on Rebecca Ostlet's doorstep, indeed, how they remain in such *excellent shape* having traveled the distance they traveled, by land and sea – and though Rebecca insists that these are Richard's eyes because she could recognize her husband's atypically large blue eyes anywhere, this is not, in Downing's view, finally the point: the young, freshly widowed botanist – for who knows what reason but likely some female complication of grief and bewilderment – is *keeping the man's eyeballs locked in her secretaire,* with her stationery and *trinkets*!

When the undertakers buried Richard, Rebecca explains to Downing, there was no wake, no open casket. Instead, when the coffin arrived in London from Africa it had been sealed shut, and was quickly laid to rest thus, unopened, at Kensal Green, and she now recalls for Downing the many complaints of the pallbearers, how 'eavy the coffin was, how it took every man on hand just to lift it, let alone to *get der bleedin' box in der ground,* and though she believed at the time that the weight borne by the coffin was – could only be – the body of her portly husband, she now wonders aloud whether maybe that was a mistake. Not to open the coffin.

Rebecca Ostlet looks at Titus Downing, and the look she gives him is pleading. 'He's been up and down Gloucester Walk for weeks,' she tells him. 'I felt I should write to you.'

Downing nods. 'I understand why you would write,' he says, gazing at Richard Ostlet's optic nerves, which are floating behind the eyeballs like tiny nervous tails. 'But, madam,' he continues, 'you are asking me to believe in ghosts, apparitions –'

'Normally, I would agree with you,' she says, and, sweeping an arm around her living room, explains that she usually keeps *plants* in the windows, but an occultist instructed her to decorate the flat with *roses* to keep Richard away, and really go overboard about it, the occultist advised, and so she went overboard. 'I have roses on the front door,' she says. 'Roses in the windows. And yet still he comes.'

'I see,' says Downing.

'I think that Richard – or whatever is remaining of Richard – wants his eyes back. I think that's why he walks. But I have no idea what to do,' Rebecca says, and smiles sadly at the Brontës, now curled in sleep at her feet.

Downing nods again, for he, fighting off his own terrible personal sadness over having lost Richard, has already formulated a plan: he explains to the woman that, quite conveniently, he has an appointment with Harold Skinner the next morning, a noted specialist in prosthetics, and if it may help her situation, with her permission, Downing would gladly *take the eyes* to Dr Skinner and ask his opinion? About what might have happened to Richard? About what to do?

With this news, a brightness overcomes Rebecca Ostlet. She declares he has her permission *indeed* and then drops the issue entirely. She begins talking about how difficult this has been for her, the *widow's obligation*, staying inside her flat all day with naught but grief; how she is, from the bottom of her soul, an *outdoors* creature, and how her terribly brief marriage commits her, in her opinion, to no further sustained isolation from society – so the dinner plans they have this evening, she says, will be followed tomorrow morning by a lecture at the Royal Institution on the remains of the Temple of Artemis at Ephesus by the discoverer himself, archaeologist John Turtle Wood, and the man started out as nothing more than an architect, does Downing know, and spent *five whole years* searching in vain before realizing there might be a paved road from the Magnesian Gate, a road leading right to the temple, which there of course *was*, six meters beneath, under sand – but at the end of her speech she inquires, and only if Downing is amenable, perhaps *he* should take the glass jar and store it in his bedroom tonight, while he is staying with her?

To all of this, Downing agrees, and later that evening, after fine roast lamb, new potatoes and two bottles of claret, when everyone has relaxed, Rebecca Ostlet, having drunk more than usual, opens up to Titus Downing about her husband: how *distant* Richard was from her almost as soon as they married. How he *traveled* all the time, and she never expected much more than a minimum of affection, but there had been no minimum of affection. 'It was like he never thought about me at all,' she says, and Downing nods, listening to Rebecca's sorrows in alternating states of amusement and pity, like he would a child explaining basic maths. Because all of this he knows already, it's internalized, and none of it he cares to hear another word about.

For no matter how many glasses of wine he drinks, Downing is not about to share with Lady Ostlet the dozens of nights he himself spent with Richard; that the two had, on many occasions, slept naked in each other's arms, or how his own thin body fit so neatly around Richard's corpulence; and Downing is certainly not going to explain how he and Richard had locked eyes at the Great Exhibition all those years ago over a small stuffed vixen, tail a-twitching; how Richard had led him down a long red-carpeted hallway and into the custodial closet where, amidst the Quick Silver, Rape Oil and Rottenstone, Ostlet kissed him with a passion Downing did not know existed in men, or how he pulled down Ostlet's trousers and took his tough, chubby cock into his mouth, and although Downing had never before allowed himself to imagine that this was what he wanted or needed, all at once it was *everything*, and he shocked himself as he realized that he knew what to do, the knowledge was innate, and when Ostlet shuddered and emptied himself into Downing's mouth, he concluded that no man ever truly loved publicly, true love was a secret, and as the two men walked back to the Exhibition, arm-brushing-arm, he saw the world very differently: that the adult human male was nothing more than a mammal in a suit, and Downing felt assured for the first time since leaving his childhood farm in Northumberland that he was Nature, and had he ever felt so like *himself*, so *awake*? — which is why he cares to hear none of Lady Ostlet's complaints, except perhaps save one:

Of course, the woman tells Downing, she was not as surprised as one might expect a wife to be upon discovering her husband's eyes stashed in a glass jar in a five-drawer specimen box from Africa because, as she's sure Downing knows (which he does), Richard suffered from exophthalmos, the *oddest* condition where the sufferer's eyes occasionally bulge out of their orbits. But what Downing may *not* know, she hiccups, is that on *certain occasions*, if Richard's head was ever violently bumped, or if his eyelids somehow turned the wrong way, his eyeballs would pop right out, secured only by their optic nerves, and it was *terrible* to witness!

Despite his cheerful disposition, Rebecca Ostlet explains, Richard suffered horribly, and the eyes were always popping out in the most inconvenient places, and a doctor had once informed him that it was called 'spontaneous globe luxation,' and there was nothing to be done but accept the fact that soon Sir Richard Ostlet would no longer be able to continue his work as a sportsman, a naturalist. The poor man, Rebecca said the doctor said, was not long from becoming completely, and irrevocably, blind.

∽

You are embracing the head of a gigantic stuffed aardvark in the back of Officer Anderson's toothy Ford Police Interceptor – wrists secured *entirely* unnecessarily in the front of your person with white plastic zip ties – crossing the Potomac to Independence Ave., right next to the Mall.

Since there are still places in the grid where nothing is working, people are outside, and these people are fat. There are fat men, fat women and fat children, and they are all wearing the same general outfit: T-shirt and shorts, white socks and sneakers. The adults themselves, they resemble large toddlers as they teeter around the Washington Monument holding $6 pretzels and tipping their phones skyward with greasy fingers as the Interceptor hurtles past L'Enfant, the Federal Center, bearing left in front of the Capitol, and Anderson *really* could have taken you to one of the substations (M Street was closer), but no: *you* go to the First District Station, that's where the chief works, and when you get there, a great wonking slab of classic DC concrete, Anderson walks you through a hallway that still smells like tobacco from cigarettes smoked over two decades ago and into a room that's right out of some movie, full of metal desks the size of baby rhinoceri and old gray desktop PCs from the Aughts.

The cops, they are actually donned in *pleated khakis*, and who even wears fucking *khakis* anymore, you think as

· 67 ·

Anderson plunks you down in a hard wooden chair and whispers to the chief the story he thinks you cannot hear but which you absolutely can.

Officer Anderson has no way of knowing that you possess incredible hearing. You've had it since birth, and it made you an extremely fussy baby, so your mother once told you, and you can hear a full conversation between two people whispering in *another room entirely,* much less just a few feet away, and the story Anderson is telling the chief is truly something: how yes, you are exactly who everyone thinks you are; how you were not only Texting While Driving you were also carrying Highly Unusual Heavy Cargo, and Officer Anderson *lifted* said Heavy Cargo from your vehicle himself and wedged it into the back seat of his Interceptor to take you both in; how, as he drove to the precinct, he observed the odd manner in which you kept one elbow *hugging* the Cargo, and Anderson just does not believe that a whole stuffed aardvark could be a *political* gift, he whispers, because a political gift would be sent to your *office,* and you had told Officer Anderson that it was sent to your *home via FedEx,* making it not a political but a *personal* gift. About this Anderson has no doubt. So, to him, the following questions remain:

Who would have personally gifted Representative Alexander Paine Wilson a gigantic stuffed aardvark? Why would the congressman have covered the head of the aardvark with a dish towel? Where was he driving the aardvark this morning, and why would he want to be rid of it?

'The whole thing *stinks,*' you hear Anderson say, and

the chief of police, a nightmarish trio of black, female and lesbian, glances at you handcuffed in your J. Crew summerwear when he says that. She asks what Anderson told you. 'The Lacey Act,' Anderson says, his brother's a hunter and knows all about the rules of game transport, and the chief laughs as she murmurs, 'Good one,' and that's when you stand up and demand to call your lawyer *immediately*; you are a congressman who has been *wrongfully arrested,* and Officer Anderson has broken all kinds of your Fourth Amendment rights, and for whatever reason, like, *has it out for you.*

You are shouting. You know that you are shouting, and you also know that it's bad to be shouting as three more cops enter, aardvark in tow.

'Thing weighs a *ton*,' they laugh and drop it loudly on a table in front of you, right there out in the open for everyone to see, and the cops in the precinct, they all get up from their desks and encircle the aardvark, air-flicking its snout and its ears, and for reasons you cannot fathom, you begin feeling slightly defensive when they snicker, calling it *crazy-weird* or *so ugly*, so you plunk back down in your seat and, wrists bound and smarting, go for your phone.

It's not in your pocket. Anderson, you remember, took your phone when you got there, and without your phone you feel naked, lonely, and you pray that your security settings were on when you texted Tampico.

'It was a *gift*,' you shout again. You cannot believe that anyone would even think you *want* this stupid aardvark! And while yes, it's true that you *did* have your elbow around it in the back of the Interceptor, it was only because the aardvark is so freaking *huge,* bulky, and the potholes in DC, as everyone knows, are no freaking *joke,* and you were just trying to keep the freaking tail of the aardvark from stabbing Officer Anderson in the head through the freaking *barrier grid* while he drove, and the snout of the aardvark from stabbing you in the groin, and you did so by embracing its head – albeit awkwardly with *your wrists freaking tied* – and as the police start writing everything down, taking your report, the police photographer comes over with an actual camera and starts snapping photos, and now there are pictures of you, pictures of you in a police station, pictures of you in a police station next to a stuffed aardvark with your wrists bound, and before your mind catches up with your body, you stand up, snatch the camera out of the photographer's hands and toss it under a desk where it breaks, and that's when the officers, clad in their khakis, fall collectively upon you.

∽

Titus Downing is on the train back to Leamington Spa. The glass jar snug in his valise holds two human eyeballs, floating like dead fish in their fluid, and he feels no guilt, none at all, for lying to Rebecca Ostlet about his reasons for departing immediately the following morning, for skipping out on the lecture on the Temple of Artemis at Ephesus, for abruptly canceling his appointment with his old roommate, noted prosthetic specialist Harold Skinner, as a new plan is already under way: Sir Richard Ostlet's eyes are *going into the aardvark,* and he knew it the first moment he saw them, for Downing, a scientist, not at all a believer in ghosts, *does* believe in coincidence; to deny coincidence is to deny *destiny,* he thinks, which is why, upon returning home to his workshop, the taxidermist carefully, using wet shellac, dips and dries each of the eyeballs several times until they are glossy, hardened, then secures them neatly, with wire and glue, in the empty eye sockets of the death mask of the gigantic, corpulent aardvark, and Downing is not at all surprised that they fit as well as they do, he works gently, in gloves with his tow forceps, as he lowers the aardvark's long-lashed lids over them, applies a wet glue from horse tooth, and though it is a gruesome and fairly macabre moment in his life, as he handles the eyes of his former lover, he cannot help but feel: *this is what love is.*

∽

'I do not like green eggs and ham,' you recite to the waiter at the Brown, Lake & Peterson Company while scrolling your phone, 'I do not like them, Sam-I-am,' and Toby Castle shoots you a glance that's like, *please.* She tosses all of her long blond hair over one shoulder and whips out: 'Because I could not stop for Death—/ He kindly stopped for me,' which is good because the waiter, like all waiters at BLPC, has 0.125% stock in the business and takes the lunchboxes and poem/menu thing very, very seriously.

He hands you your paper menu delicately, like you might stain it.

'I'm sorry, I was in jail today,' you say, and Toby Castle shoots the waiter an apologetic look, like the two of you have already been married for years, and sighs as she says, all dispirited, 'I'm just getting a salad.'

Toby got dispirited the moment she saw you looking disheveled at the bar of the restaurant, the moment you told her what happened this morning, how you were brought downtown to an actual fucking police precinct and spent all day there, and how they are now investigating the gift of a stuffed aardvark – and it *was* just a gift – which arrived on your doorstep from you have no idea who.

You can't say you blame her; after all, she really took her time getting ready and looks pretty and fresh in a pale blue and expensive-looking silk dress that is perfect for the heat, she's done it all, heels, hair and makeup, and here you are across the table, covered in sweat, your J. Crew all wrinkled – but it doesn't matter how good she looks, you want to convey, she's damned *lucky* to have you sitting across from her, you think, given who you are, given where you've been all day. (This is not what you tell her.)

'It was all a big misunderstanding,' you say, tearing into some free corned beef eggrolls that the waiter has placed on your table in a Trixie Collins lunchbox, and it does not go without your attention that around you, your peers are eating out of vintage Batmans, vintage Spider-Mans, Supermans, Aquamans, and Green Lanterns, but you didn't get any of those lunchboxes. The waiter, pissed off at your poem, has given you Trixie Collins.

'Who the hell is Trixie Collins,' you say to the waiter,

who's now at the next table, and he just looks at you, scowls, and mouths, *google it*.

'*Anyway,*' you say, 'the officer did not and does not understand the Lacey Act, and any time a cop wants to go up against me in terms of who knows their statutes, I just say: bring it.'

'What is the Lacey Act,' Toby Castle says, and it's her most bored voice ever.

'The Lacey Act,' you explain, paraphrasing what cursory info you gleaned from your phone before Anderson took it, 'was, like, *established in 1900* to prevent poachers from transporting birds and animals and plants and all kinds of wildlife – basically anything living – across state lines. Now it's, like, *illegal* to import or export an animal or, in this case, send illegally poached big game to taxidermists.'

'So your aardvark was illegally poached.'

'It's not *my* aardvark,' you say as you watch Toby Castle examining her egg roll, flicking off the fatty bits with her manicured fingernails, and really wish she'd, like, *make more of an effort* because there are 1267 unread text messages and 899 unread emails on your phone, and Nancy Fucking Beavers is right on your heels, you have *work to do* for Chrissakes, but here you are at this dumbass restaurant, and it's all for her and she *doesn't care,* and you are beginning to wonder if the idea about Finding A Wife isn't totally stupid after all when Toby says, 'Let's just drop it,' snaps her fingers, and orders from the waiter two gin and mashed cucumber gimlets, which instantly helps.

You apologize. You tell Toby how great she looks, you just didn't expect to spend the day in a police precinct. It took your staffers another three hours to deal with the paperwork, get back your phone, and it's all you can do right now to deal with the fact that tomorrow's headline all over the world is going to read something akin to REPRESENTATIVE ALEX WILSON (R) ARRESTED FOR ILLEGAL POSSESSION OF TAXIDERMIED AARDVARK, and despite the fact that you're totally innocent, you say, it's going to be hell on Earth for your staffers if it isn't already.

You hold up your phone. You show Toby Castle all of your unread messages, and Toby smiles at you, and what she says next is the reason you like this girl.

'That's *tomorrow,*' she says, sliding her hands over the table, fingering the buttons on your wrinkled cuffs. 'Not tonight,' and it's clear then and there that you are going to bring Toby back to your place and you both are going to take a steam shower underneath your Kohler Vibrant Brushed Bronze WaterTile Ambient Rain Overhead Rain Shower showerhead and you are going to make up for this god-awful day by fucking the living daylights – if you can – out of Brian Castle's daughter.

∽

'Come View the Aardvark,' Downing writes to museums, to reporters, 'with the ears of a rabbit and a snout like a pig's, a kangaroo tail, and one can hardly believe it exists! The specimen, I believe, is large for its genus, weighs as much as a small human woman, and possesses a unique *esprit* that can only be believed when seen.'

The day of the Viewing is scheduled for Saturday next, Titus Downing's forty-first birthday, and although he never can tell how a Viewing will go, although the aardvark is neither as tall as the giraffe nor anywhere near as impressive-looking, he believes that when the Viewers catch one glimpse of its *stance*, its *personality*, they will see what he sees: a peculiar, melancholic kind of beauty, and it is because of this belief – coupled with Walter Potter's immense popularity, which now demands from Downing a bare minimum of publicity, what he calls 'The Debasement' – that over the course of the next week, on top of the personal letters to museums, reporters, all the paid advertisements he writes, the taxidermist will hire a small theater troupe for the day of the Viewing to, while wearing homemade aardvark costumes, *mimic the actions of the aardvark*. And he, Downing, will stiffly show the actors himself, with his own crooked body, how the creature might amble the plains of the Karoo beds in southern Africa, backed by distant mountains. How it might, as it ambles, quickly tamp its odd, piggy snout into dirt, and the boys will all practice crawling around, tossing their heads, and they will make for themselves from drawings created in Downing's own hand papier-mâché snouts for their noses, long ears for their heads, spoony claws for their hands, and, for the backs of their trousers, heavy kangaroo tails.

The only thing Downing does not advertise is the eyes, for he knows they will be the surprise, the real spectacle, because he has done something which no taxidermist has ever before done, and everyone will look into the aardvark's eyes and feel what he feels (*love*), but they will not be able to put their finger on why, or what it is that makes them feel so – and as Downing completes the mannequin and polishes for the last time the aardvark's heavy wooden mount, quite pleased with his choice of Leadwood, the finest *Combretum imberbe* imported from the aardvark's natural habitat, he regards the blue eyes of the aardvark and recalls the last time he and Richard Ostlet saw one another, just one week before Richard departed for Africa.

There was nothing particularly different that day. Seeing Richard was exactly like it always was: as though no time had passed between that moment and two and a half decades ago in the custodial closet at the Great Exhibition. Except Ostlet wasn't well.

'Nerves,' he had said, but there was something more. Downing had looked into Ostlet's big round eyes – Rebecca was not joking about the bulge and slippage of Ostlet's bright blue oculi – and he remembers now how Richard confessed that he was having trouble sleeping; that his eyes would *stay open, all on their own,* and if he weren't so tired all the time he would maybe mind slightly less, but along with the fatigue and the headaches was the truth about his imminent blindness, his vision had been failing for some time now, and in England it was one thing, but he was worried about what it might mean in Africa.

Downing had laid his thin arm over Ostlet's chest, roiled his chest hair around a long finger. 'You need an *assistant,*' he said, and offered to join Ostlet on his trip, if he pleased. He suggested that the two might have a *grand time* in Africa, that he could assist Richard in any way he needed assisting, that he not only could take his dictation but he might help him, well, *relax*, and it was then that Ostlet inexplicably had jumped up from Downing's bed.

He said that he was sorry, he just remembered an important appointment he was already late for and assured Titus that he would call upon him next week, before leaving, and as Downing watched his lover hastily dress in the moonlight, he understood at once that he had lost him.

Downing already knew about the woman, the former student, the pretty, young botanist living in London, and as he heard Ostlet hurry out the door and down the stairs, through his taxidermy shop, as the front door jingled merrily as Ostlet let himself out, Titus Downing spread his lithe, naked body over the warm place on his bed where Ostlet had been and smelled for the last time his scent on the sheets, and it's why the taxidermist has been, in the months ever since, afflicted: the melancholy of the sudden departure of his lover has been *almost unbearable*; without Richard Ostlet, Titus Downing had left in his life only a lost brother working unceremoniously in the Outer Hebrides. A poor mother and poor father running their farm in Northumberland, who were themselves at death's door – he was alone.

Downing, who had never before been presented with the opportunity to grieve for love, wept for Ostlet that night as though for all mankind, and he *could not have known* that for all his weeping, weeks later, a large aardvark in Africa would send her tongue, long as rope, into a tunnel, licking up termites, feeling them pepper her thick whiskers, which protected her eyes, nose and mouth like small quills; that she would walk daintily, but not unsteadily, on the extremities of her digits, head inclined, snout brushing the sweet dirt on the ground; and that she would embark thusly, alone – for aardvarks always travel alone – upon a miles-long journey into the dark African night, looking for more food, stopping only to listen for occasional threats until she found herself facing a handsome and clever African hunter that she had not, despite her long ears, heard coming.

For if the aardvark *had* heard the lightest rustle, she would have easily thrown herself into a tunnel or quickly dug for herself a hiding place, a defensive burrow, but the hunter was already in the bush, lance at the ready, and the gigantic aardvark, ears slung back, tail heavy as a sack, felt the shock of pain as the lance entered her side, tore through her heart, lungs and stomach, and only then did she dive deep into a tunnel, bleeding obscenely.

The aardvark thrust her spoony claws into the ground like two anchors, forcing the hunter to enter the tunnel in darkness, groping, swiping termites off his arms, crying out from their bites, sneezing them out of his nose until at last he heard her grunting in pain and somehow grasped her thick tail, and it was *hours* of pulling the wounded aardvark out from her habitat, a kind of pulling not at all unlike a fisherman working a big fish from the sea, and when the hunter at last succeeded it was not for any talent on his part; the aardvark had lost too much blood. She was weak, her grip on the earth had become loose, untenable, and when the hunter yanked her tail with his full strength and the aardvark finally emerged from the hole in the ground, she was long past afraid and half-conscious.

Overnight, she was carried in a canvas hammocked between two hunters' shoulders, cradled on her back, her front legs – plantigrade – hanging over the sides, her hind legs – digitigrade – sticking up toward the sky, and though he couldn't have imagined it then, Downing imagined it now: how the aardvark was presented this way to Ostlet.

He imagined Richard fussing with his glasses, trying in vain to see as much of the aardvark as possible but relying, in the end, on the eyes of his young assistant, a student of his in the Department of Naturalism at Edinburgh who, the following evening, after the aardvark was respectfully slaughtered, her carcass hung, after her bones were boiled and all was wrapped up in a brown paper package and prepared for Titus Downing, rebuffed the advances of a man fifty years old and nearly blind.

Perhaps, Downing guessed, it was regret at his decision *not* to bring Titus with him after all that Richard, blind and alone, took his own life, and so preoccupied is he with the thought as he completes the aardvark and turns off the gaslight, as he walks upstairs and puts himself to bed, that he does not tend to the strange, dark figure which, in the minutes since, has appeared outside his shopwindow, pacing to and fro underneath the twelve stag heads.

∽

After you and Toby agreed to bail on dinner, you paid the check, went to your Tahoe, climbed up into the two front seats, and started making out. You both went crazy, groping at each other's faces, and though you knew reporters would be looking for you, you have no idea how they could have found you so quickly, that they would have been hiding around the corner of the Brown, Lake & Peterson Company, but they are here, a huge buzzing number of newspaper reporters, assorted paparazzi, and when they start shouting, when their lights start flashing, Toby screams and you panic, throw the Tahoe into gear and take off down the street.

'*Slow down,* you're just making it look *worse,*' Toby is yelling, and you're yelling back, 'Shut up, I know what I'm doing. *Who's* in the public eye? *Who?!*'

And that shuts up Toby Castle. At least until you reach Asher Place when more photographers, upon seeing your Tahoe, spill out of the children's playground like termites from old wood. And it's not even remotely like you have seen in old movies with guys in nice suits holding cameras with great popping bulbs; these guys are in fucking *tracksuits* – cheap-ass shiny *tracksuits* – holding cheap gym bags from Target, and all their money has gone into expensive digital shutter cameras, pepper spray in their bags, and Toby screams again when one of them jumps in front of your car and starts shouting, 'Alex! Congressman Wilson!' and flashes away, and before you get inside the garage of 2486 Asher, they're flashing up the back of the Tahoe.

'The aardvark!' one shouts, like it's Beyoncé or

something, and you nearly run a guy down as you punch the garage door opener, press the gas pedal, and careen the Tahoe into its parking space. When you're in, you punch the opener again like you hate it.

'Jesus Fucking Christ!' shouts Toby.

'I know,' you say. But you're home now. 'It's over,' you say.

You apologize to Toby for how crazy it is out there and swear that this will all pass soon, and you are really glad she is with you tonight, and as you say these things to the girl Toby Castle you realize that you are starting to believe them.

'Not *them*,' Toby says. 'You! What's in the back, Alex? Is that the fucking aardvark?'

Why yes, it is indeed the fucking aardvark, you explain, and the cops have allowed you to keep it until the permit business is cleared up, and what's the big deal? It's stuffed!

You are lying. You understand more than she does that this *is* a big deal, that all Officer Anderson has to do now is find the FedEx man who delivered the aardvark to your house to get the name Gregory Tampico, and there is, let's face it, a very *solid* chance that Anderson will find the name because he has already *asked you* to produce the FedEx number that came with the delivery, though he knows that you're not about to give it up to him – Well *golly,* you appear to have lost it, you'll say – and that's when Officer Anderson will start making inquiries at the FedEx main office about *routes,* about certain glasses-wearing, beard-sporting delivery drivers, and as you lead Toby Castle up from the confines of the garage and into your townhouse, you suddenly feel desperately unsafe, like, *it's so not okay* to leave the aardvark in the Tahoe because you haven't had a chance to fully inspect it, and what if Greg Tampico had actually stuffed something inside the aardvark? What if one of the paparazzi breaks in and finds it?

You are panicking. You know this.

You know that you are panicking.

You grab a flashlight off a shelf and tell Toby to go upstairs without you, you'll be there in a minute, and you return to the garage, open the rear of the Tahoe, and turn on the flashlight.

The aardvark's pale fur glistens in bright light and covers a thick, yellow-pink hide. Its long ears are silky, smooth as copier paper, and the snout, although toughened with age, is still rubbery. You feel under its belly for a seam, or something unusual, but there is nothing unusual. Quite the opposite, as you stroke the aardvark, you admit that it feels quite *pleasurable* actually, and this surprises you, slightly unsettles you, and you begin to understand why Greg Tampico liked it so much: from a distance, the aardvark is horrible-looking, but up close it's actually a pretty nice animal and it makes you feel weirdly *good* all of a sudden: the look on its face with its head all downturned, askance, is not *ugly* at all, it's *coy* – and you actually smile a little bit as you run your hands between its soft ears, over its forehead, and gaze into its eyes, but when you do this, your hands stop.

You shine the light into the eyes of the aardvark, which are, you wonder – blue?

They are. The eyes are definitely blue, and you have

never heard of a *blue-eyed aardvark* before, nor with it felt the tremor of recognition that you feel now.

It's *déjà vu*, like you are seeing something emotionally familiar that is intellectually unfamiliar, and you wonder while standing there downstairs in your dark, hot garage with Toby Castle already disrobing in your bathroom upstairs, brushing her teeth, checking her underwear, her hair, scent and makeup, preening herself for intercourse – how this is possible when most mammals in nature, you recall from Ms Sline, have *brown eyes*, so these blue eyes must be some kind of *anomaly*, but how they *do* make the aardvark look familiar, you think, as though bearing some kind of consciousness. But what *kind*?

Alan Brickmann. You were ten, Alan Brickmann was twelve, a neighbor of yours for only nine months before his family moved to some landlocked place called Grand Island, Nebraska. There was a high cotton hammock in his backyard, slung too high by his father so you had to climb the trunk of the tree in bare feet to get there, but once ensconced you were quiet, unseen, and Alan Brickmann, a constellation of zits on his forehead, pushed your toes with his toes. He said you should practice kissing, and as you began, he did not say anything else. Your hands touched his body, moving in circles over his clothes as you kissed like you knew what you were doing, but somehow you did, the knowledge was innate (it was not on TV), though it only lasted a moment before Alan unzipped himself and brought out his dick in his palm, and there, in the soft dusk-light, it looked like he was holding three marshmallows.

You said no, that was *gross*, and got out of there, you ran home, and now in the darkness of your garage at 2486 Asher Place with paparazzi outside, Toby Castle upstairs, the sadness about Alan Brickmann which the aardvark's expression has somehow evoked? It surprises you. It's an old weight, one that you've carried for twenty-five years that you thought you'd forgotten about, yet now blooms in your chest like a newly sprung fungus, and all you can do with it is attempt to share it with someone, split it.

But the only person with whom you might possibly split it, you think as you reluctantly close the rear doors of the Tahoe and lock it, is not even close to the person you wish.

∽

It is five days before the Viewing. A hot August night. A round moon shines morosely over the River Leam, the body of water which glides from Northamptonshire to Warwickshire, lulling to sleep every night the near twenty thousand who still populate the sleepy in-between town of Royal Leamington Spa.

Titus Downing, alone in his bedroom, can hear the river moving. He is not sleeping. He is brightly awake, lying on top of his bed in his underclothes, for it is much too hot to lie anywhere else, and Downing's bed is a large four-poster over which he hung long aubergine velvet curtains the day it was bought. When he touches the curtains, they remind him that although he is not rich, he is not poor like his parents in Northumberland.

Tonight, the curtains are wide open, and though he is feeling confident about the aardvark, about the events to come, nights before Viewings are always a torment to Downing. Every outside noise vexes the senses. Downing knows that he will not sleep and listens unhappily to the steady rush of water flowing from the weir of Jephson Gardens, the lone *baroo* of a hound, the steady *clop* of the horses on cobblestones, the sporadic profanities from drunks as they sing, swinging themselves around the stone columns of the Royal Pump Rooms and Baths, Leamington Spa's famous old pools once filled with healing waters which, it turned out, did not heal anyone.

Downing would perhaps be more at ease were it not for the letter he received two days ago from Rebecca Ostlet.

Lady Ostlet read about the Viewing in the London papers, she has written, and given that she never got to thank Downing in person for assisting her at a time when she most needed assistance, and given that the beast, the *Orycteropus afer*, was the last procured by her husband – whose 'essence' now has, by the by, at last departed from Gloucester Walk – she has decided that she would rather like to see the so-called 'aardvark' for herself, and Downing should thus prepare for her coming, and postscript: might there be space for the Brontës?

Downing changes position several times in his bed, worrying about Rebecca Ostlet, her three feathery dogs, and whatever else the woman might bring with her.

Because although many women came to View Downing's giraffe, the giraffe was obviously too big to be Viewed *inside* the shop, and so it was presented *outside,* and it occurs to Downing now, in his bed, that no woman has ever before actually crossed the threshold *into* his taxidermy shop, and any previous delight imagining women fainting in front of the aardvark is now replaced by the knowledge that they will be *inside his shop to see it,* and Downing decides that while he has rather less concern about the rest of them, he cannot shake the image of pretty, thin-waisted *Lady Ostlet* running her delicate woman fingers over his animal hides, picking up his glues or his brushes or calipers – and he imagines her handling his prized Currier knife, his glass bottles of lacquer, his Essence of Pearl, and by god, if it takes a while for Downing to return to an animal's *jiva* when he is disturbed by a delivery boy, then *heaven knows how long it will take* for his shop to feel like his own again once the woman's passed through it.

The thought disturbs him so deeply that by twenty past ten, Downing can bear it no longer, leaps from his canopied bed and travels downstairs to the kitchen for a bit of food. He removes from his pantry a pouch of crackers, a jar of some potted meat, and while leaning against the pantry door, nauseously nibbling his victuals, he hears the slow shuffle of a drunk outside his front door.

It is not the first time the drunks of Leamington have wandered away from the river. Grown men will, occasionally, sleep on his doorstep under the stag heads, sometimes all the way through until morning, so Titus Downing listens, waiting for the sound of a man collapsing against his front door, the sound he's heard often, but there is no such sound. The drunk man keeps walking. And the walking sounds *odd,* as though he is dragging something behind him, and a shiver travels through Titus Downing.

He listens as the walker grows distant, waits for the man to disappear completely, for when he disappears completely Downing will return upstairs to bed – so it is to Downing's great unease that the sound does *not* disappear, and instead, grows louder. The drunk man, he gathers, has *turned back around*. In no time, he is walking again in front of the shop, and then again: silence.

What can Downing do in his little dark kitchen?

When the sound picks up once more, and it is a very *distinctive* echo of heel-sole swiping stone, he knows at once that he has heard it before, that this is no drunk; that whenever his friend departed this flat late at night there was *always* the door's jingle of sleigh bells followed by this same music, and he is *certain* that Richard Ostlet's footsteps are the footsteps he hears now, sweeping the streets in his leather Wellington boots, which he wore day and night, uneven in rhythm for his uncertain steps – it's the eyes, nyctalopia's to blame – and Downing, who has not for a moment forgotten what Rebecca told him about seeing Richard walking to and fro in front of their home on Gloucester Walk, is now frozen stiff in the pantry, his head low, his hands pressed against the closed wooden doors, and he is waiting for the apparition to tire of its walking and move on, and Downing will stay there all night if he has to, because: fear! In a flood at his throat!

He cannot make himself move or walk to the front of the shop and stand in the shadows of his stuffed beasts and see with his own eyes the ghost that he knows is there, its ethereal hands pressed against the window-panes, its bandaged face affixed toward the back workshop because the door has been left open, and where, upon a workbench, a big stuffed *Orycteropus afer* is clearly visible, herself frozen in the walking position, her right hoof-claw lifted, her head hung low, her long ears raised and alert as she shows off her new bright blue eyes, shellacked to a shine!

Over the eyes hang the thick eyelids of the aardvark, the lashes of which Downing each positioned just this morning with small tweezers so as to make her look *coy* to her Viewers, flirtatious, and Downing has no choice but to wait in this manner for the moment when Ostlet – or whatever remains of Ostlet – at last *moves on* from the shop, his Wellingtons shuffling off this time for good.

It is only then that Downing summons the courage to slip into the workshop. He procures from under his nightshirt the brass key which he wears at all times on a lanyard, to securely lock the workshop door, and, hands shaking, he locks it.

∽

It is Monday morning. Congress is not back in session. You are not back in session. You are sitting up naked in bed with Toby Castle, and both of your laptops are open like great, glowing mouths, your legs still entwined underneath your 1200-thread-count Sferra Milos bone-colored sheets ($1695) as you pick up your phone.

Although Fox shuttered the story, you have now 2345 unread text messages and 3509 unread emails as it appears Nancy Fucking Beavers has pounced:

REPRESENTATIVE ALEXANDER P. WILSON (R) ARRESTED, the *Washington Post* declares, the *New York Times* declares, the *Wall Street Journal* declares, the *LA Times*, the *Boston Globe*, the *Chicago Tribune*, CNN, NBC, HuffPost and Google News and even the BBC and the *Guardian* all declare, and you have four hashtags trending on Twitter, the cruelest of which is *#cancelWilson*. Fox and its minor sycophantic affiliates, thank god, are reporting on a rhesus monkey who flung shit on a Democrat from Wisconsin at the Sacramento Zoo – but other than that, pictures of the aardvark which the police took at the station, which the reporters took of the back of your Tahoe, they are everywhere, and then suddenly it's pictures of the aardvark alternating with pictures of the front door of 2486 Asher Place – Ralph Lauren 'British Racing Car' green with a Victorian brass lion's-head knocker – which is your front door.

You turn on your 75-inch Samsung widescreen 4K Q9F Series UHD TV with HDR ($3999) in your bedroom and watch as the middle-aged brunette in a marigold pantsuit, hair cut short and sprayed into a brown carapace, barks into a microphone:

'I am not interested in discussing Alex Wilson's personal life. That's discourse beneath my campaign. But we all know Congressman Wilson is known for his extravagant taste, and if he wishes to furnish his extravagant home with taxidermy, it is his choice, as an American, to do so. In the end, it is the voters who will decide whether or not they want to keep in office a congressman who himself keeps an endangered species as a decorative ornament.'

You immediately google *is aardvark endangered?* and learn that there's actually such a thing as an Endangerment Rating and the aardvark has a risk of endangerment of 'Least Concern,' and the sturdy-ass mammal has fucking trucked around Earth for a fucking *infinity* before human beings, its origins are fucking Mesozoic, it *never evolved*, and it is actually one of the least endangered mammals on the planet!

Human beings will all kill each other and die off, and millions of other creatures will each in their own way and time die off, but the aardvark will probably *never* die off, and knowing this makes you furious – not because it awakens within you some humble cognizance of your own pointless, mortal frailty (which it does) but because Nancy Fucking Beavers has so obviously planted this little lie to goad you, put you on the defensive, to make you talk about the aardvark, and the very last thing you want to do right now is talk about the aardvark.

'Just get rid of it,' Toby says, and blinks bigly. 'Dump it in the Potomac. Say that you lost it.'

Toby's trying to look smart but she just looks pretty, and she hasn't even brushed her teeth but she *smells* pretty, you think, unlike Greg Tampico, who always woke up smelling warm and weird, like undercooked beef, and as you are quietly admitting to yourself that you *so* preferred Greg Tampico's meat-scent to Toby Castle's perfume, the way out of this mess beautifully horizons across your frontal lobe:

You and Toby Castle will get dressed in something clean. Relaxed-looking. Like you've been away somewhere beachy. For the weekend. You will open the green door downstairs and hold each other, waving to the reporters, and grinning, you will kiss each other and wave some more. And then you will announce your engagement.

The aardvark, you will publicly share, was an ill-conceived *engagement gift*, nothing more, one which you have been advised to return, but one which you're considering keeping because you – unlike *Mrs Beavers*, you will say – *you* are actually In Office; you would rather your time be spent working for The People of the Great State of Virginia, and you are, right at this moment, working on Jobs – and you want to *give* The People the chance to seek out and buy their *own* healthcare coverage because of *dignity*, because Ronald Reagan was right when he said, 'Government's first duty is to protect the people, not run their lives,' and look what happens when we get things for free, haha!

Then you'll deliver a strangled chiasmus which is nonsense but sounds good, a line your staffers were saving for your next debate: 'After all, no one can help what is given to them, but they can give help to others,' and then, in a sugary voice, 'Toby reminds me of this *every day*,' you'll say and beam, and in that moment, your reelection campaign will officially launch.

You have climbed up onto your knees. Your naked body is wrapped all Grecian-like in your beautiful bedsheets, and

you have grabbed Toby's hands, which are light as crois-
sants. 'Marry me,' you say, and your eyebrows lift in a playful
manner you mastered at prep school, no woman can ever
resist it, and it got you through English and Calculus, several truancies, a graffiti incident, and once even a student
integrity panel in which a boy accused you of assaulting
him, but you got off because he was a fat kid and it was the
Nineties.

There are no exclamations of joy.

Toby looks startled maybe but not in the least bit surprised. She looks at you like you're crazy at first, but it's just
an act; she knows perfectly well what you're up to because
as soon as she gets it, she smiles and starts laughing, which
is why you totally, hands-down adore Toby Castle.

'Even better!' she shouts, and jumps out of bed.

Toby tells you to hurry. Get dressed. She'll be downstairs in a minute, she says, she only needs to borrow some
khakis, one of your white button-downs, and she can
accessorize with the earrings she wore last night, she says,
and yeah, it will be really cute if she looks boyish, tousled,
'like Jackie O fresh off a yacht or something,' she says, and
you put yourself completely in her hands when you toss
her the clothes. Except for the khakis.

'I don't own any khakis,' you say.

'Something else, then,' she says.

You throw her some dark blue CK close-fitting silk-
blend men's trousers ($460).

As for you, for this occasion, you also dress yourself in
CK: the same trousers in brown, a pink gingham shirt
($210), a white leather belt ($184), and you deliberately

don't button the collar as you run downstairs in bare feet, excited, when the landline rings.

You would not even *have* a landline if it were not for your mother. She is the only one who ever uses it, and she insists on you having a landline because she is old and does not trust cell phones.

'Who's that?' Toby shouts.

'It's my mother,' you shout back, and pick up the phone.

It's not your mother.

'Wilson,' a voice says.

'Who is this,' you say as Toby Castle starts working your hair dryer upstairs, a black and red MANGROOMER 1680XL-6 Professional Ionic Hair Dryer for Men ($179), which is weird, you think, because her hair is already dry.

'*Who is this,*' you say again, and sit down on the canary-yellow velvet Victorian sofa, *Images of Greatness* still spread-eagled on the coffee table, opened to a photo of Ronald Reagan and Pope John Paul II in Miami, perched in these two really beautiful Arabian-looking fabric chairs –

'Do me a favor,' the voice says, and it's a man's voice. 'Is your internet working?'

'It is,' you say.

'I'm sending you something. Check your email.'

You pick up your real phone, and there at the top of your now 4333 unread emails is an email from an undisclosed sender. All it says is *Herero*.

'Are you Herero?' you say, and the voice only says to look at the picture, closely, so you look at the picture.

It's a vintage black-and-white photograph of some kind of big old hunting lodge with wide picnic tables. The lodge is literally the size of a movie theater, and there's a big stone chimney that rises up between small windows of colored glass, and the glass, set in lead, glows over a vast amalgamation of furs, of objets d'art, of china, jewels, and silver tea settings, and it all looks pilfered, like some kind of booty, and also on the walls, covering the tables, a riot of taxidermy: stuffed geese and stuffed ducks, a sour-faced raccoon, a big open-mouthed leopard, a snarling baboon, numerous stoic elk heads, and there's even an entire eagle, wide-winged, captured frozen in flight.

Underneath the eagle, on the floor and toward the right side, a large stuffed aardvark is mounted on a sturdy block of wood. Its head is slightly lowered, its long ears alert, looking askance at the photographer with one of its claws gently raised, and at the very bottom of the photograph, handwritten, is the purported date and location: *1944, Reichsjägerhof Rominten.*

'The aardvark,' you say, and the man confirms that yes, that is the aardvark. But that is not all.

'*What* then,' you say.

'This is the hunting lodge of Hermann Göring.'

'Göring,' you say, like it's a nonsense word. 'Göring. Göring like the Nazi Göring?'

'Not *like* the Nazi,' the man says. 'The aardvark belonged to Hermann Göring's father, Heinrich. Heinrich Göring was the first governor-general of the German Protectorate of South West Africa. What is now known as Namibia.'

'Namibia,' you say.

'He was the leader of the "Schutztruppe," the German troops who killed the Herero and the Namaqua people in what is broadly understood to be the century's first genocide. Heinrich gave the aardvark to Hermann as a present when he graduated from a military academy in Lichterfelde –'

My god, you are thinking as the man is speaking, *Tampico's aardvark's a Nazi,* and try to locate the man's voice – you swear you've heard it before but cannot, for the life of you, place it! 'Seriously,' you say, 'who *is* this,' and that's when Toby Castle swoops downstairs looking refreshed and adorable.

She asks who you're talking to, and the man, having heard her, hangs up.

'What's wrong,' Toby asks, fussing an earring.

'Nothing,' you say, standing up from the sofa. You smile. You squeeze Toby's hands, take her by the elbow, and together you open your green front door with the brass lion's-head knocker and, waving to the horde of reporters, the entire American public, you make your announcement:

'The cat's out of the bag,' you say, grinning, waving. 'The aardvark was an engagement gift, nothing more,' you explain, it was all a big misunderstanding, and everyone should calm down because everything's *fine,* everything is going to be just *fine,* then you kiss Toby Castle's cheek all sheepish, welcoming the simultaneous flash and shutter of a thousand small-format, weather-resistant, pro-digital Canons which are currently eclipsing the children's playground, at the center of which, dangling precariously from his knees on the monkey bars, is the chubby black boy from yesterday who, unbeknownst to you, lingered on your stoop after you closed the door in his face, caught for himself a glimpse of the aardvark, and now knows exactly what he needs to do to see it.

∽

'Ladies and Gentlemen, come View Titus Downing's new masterpiece! The African Aardvark! For One Night Only! Available Only to Those Bold Enough to Participate!' the *Evening Standard* declares, and although Downing once recreated an entire giraffe, capturing its exact *jiva*, making everyone who saw the giraffe *feel like a giraffe*, feel the lanky swing of its neck, the long teeth reaching for acacia leaves, the stiff knuckle joints of its knees, that is *nothing*, the paper goes on to say, compared to what the people will feel when they at long last cast their eyes upon the aardvark.

In the few days that have passed since Downing first heard the slow shuffle of what he imagined to be Sir Richard Ostlet under the antlers of stags, he has been hard at work readying his shop for the Viewing, which means:

Rolling up the Bengal tiger skin into one huge, fat, furry scroll and storing it in an equally fat wooden barrel. Cleaning and oiling the battered pine workbenches, organizing scattered brushes, polishing all knives, scissors, even tweezers of various lengths and points. Then it's wiping dust from glass bottles of fluids, sweeping and scrubbing the floors, washing all windows, and Downing does all of this himself before arranging in his main shop-window the finest of his own personal collection, and these are four stuffed geese, three stuffed dogs, assorted stuffed fish and stuffed rabbits, and a collection of skittish-looking brocks and tods, in the center of which Downing places his personal favorite, a memento from the Hyde Park Exhibition: the shining taupe vixen with an elegant, upturned snout.

The gathering of tods are arranged around the vixen so it appears they protect her – which Downing believes the women will enjoy – and when it's ready, when all is complete, the taxidermist returns to his workshop to occupy himself for the day with a small commission from a local family.

On the menu is an amiable coal-black Schipperke, a decade-old lapdog with a tail like a chimney brush and ears like a bat's, and although Downing is usually bored by such commissions, little dead dogs have kept him in business these some twenty years, and he has stuffed more lapdogs than perhaps any other creature, so for him the friendly Schipperke is just the sort of mindless distraction he needs to avoid thinking about the Viewing tomorrow, about the hordes of reporters and collectors and smatterings of people who represent the General Public – or about the arrival of Rebecca Ostlet, who, Downing is now convinced, will traipse through his shop before Viewing the aardvark, talking about, sure, how fine and noble the creatures in the windows all look, but will, in time, under her breath whisper what all women whisper: *'He's still no*

Walter Potter!' – and the Schipperke helps Downing not worry about Walter Potter or how much money he makes, but most of all, the little black dog helps Downing avoid thinking about the undeniable fact that he has actually seen, in broad daylight, the body of Sir Richard Ostlet walking past his shop three times now, eyes bandaged, Wellingtons *scha-lump*ing.

Downing, the scientist, intellectually cannot bring himself to believe what his own eyes have seen, not even when lunchtime arrives and, as he is brushing the playful culottes of the Schipperke, his neck hairs start tingling. Not even when he senses that the Wellingtons are, once again, parked in front of the shop. Which they are.

Outside, Sir Richard Ostlet's bandaged face has arranged itself in the center of the taxidermist's shopwindow, positioned right in front of the vixen, and Downing, still in his workshop bent over the dog, cannot bring himself to acknowledge even the remote possibility that the being *out there* is otherworldly. For although he, like any educated man, has read his Voltaire and agrees that 'everything in nature is resurrection,' and has even entertained the likelihood that he has been here, as Goethe declared himself to be, 'a thousand times before,' and Downing, if asked, could repeat on cue from Moore's famous poem *Lalla Rookh*: 'From frame to frame the unextinguish'd soul / Rapidly passes, till it reach the goal!' – he too, like any educated man, well knows that reincarnation is not *magic*, the boundaries are set, the *jiva* is either *samsara* (trapped) or *moksha* (liberated), and though most souls are doomed to repeat themselves endlessly to shed their heavy layers of *karma,* the *jiva,* the soul, the what-have-you, the eternal life-essence? – it is not bloody *magic,* and Downing has utterly no patience for people who believe in ghosts, apparitions, and instead he believes that what lives on this cold Earth is everything, there is nothing more until death, at which point life, it may just return again as it seems to in taxidermy, and to be frank, Downing is rather looking forward to the whole aardvark business ending if truth be told, so the aardvark will become another man's problem, so this 'essence' might follow the aardvark to another town, chasing his eyes across another land, and Downing himself might close his shop, retire to his father's farm in Northumberland, leaving Royal Leamington Spa, to become what, deep down, Downing has always known he was: a simple farmer.

All of which is why Downing ignores the figure standing outside and sets his mind on tilling fields as he shapes the pink anus of the Schipperke, holding its tail, and it's why, if he hears the sleigh bells jingle, he ignores them.

It is why he ignores the figure as it enters the shop, walks slowly toward the back room, and opens the creaking door, ignores it even as it stands – as it is standing right now – so closely behind Titus Downing, leaning its chest upon his thin, bird-like shoulder blades, breathing a human man's breath, warm and wet, onto the back of his neck.

∽

You cannot know that Brian Castle, Toby's tech-billionaire father, is watching CNN when he sees his only daughter holding your arm, grinning and waving at cameras. You cannot know that upon seeing this, the ticker flashing CONGRESSMAN ALEX WILSON AND BRIAN CASTLE'S DAUGHTER ENGAGED, the man sits up straight at his desk and goes, 'Shit.' That he picks up his phone. That he has been reading the news and knows all about your arrest, your illegal possession of a taxidermied aardvark, and he has never liked you, has never liked politicians in general, of any makeup or breed, and so he is going to put an end to all this immediately. All he needs is some dirt on Wilson and he cannot imagine that it will be difficult to find, and it is not difficult to find.

The news gave up the name of the arresting officer, Officer Ernest Quinlan Anderson, and how easy is it to learn that Officer Anderson works at the First District Station, and Brian Castle can get ahold of pretty much anyone he wants to, and in less than four minutes he gets ahold of Officer Anderson.

'Ernie Anderson,' says Officer Anderson, when he picks up the phone.

Brian Castle, sixty-one and for ten long years a skin cancer survivor, is not a man who wastes time. He wants to speak about the aardvark, where Anderson thinks Wilson got it, but Anderson says he can't say much other than what the papers have already reported: the aardvark was delivered to Congressman Wilson via FedEx, and he's been on the phone all morning with FedEx.

'I don't suppose you can tell me if you found anything,' Brian Castle asks, and Anderson, axe for Wilson still grinding, confesses that he has found little so far because Wilson's phone, it was totally locked, and all he knows is that the delivery was made to 2486 Asher Place yesterday morning, August 2nd. Although Wilson *said* it was FedEx, FedEx cannot seem to locate the driver, Anderson says. Nor can they even locate the twelve-digit FedEx number, which is strange – and the package *might* have been deposited in person at the night drop-off on Eisenhower Avenue in Alexandria, he says, the only FedEx shipping center which allows such large in-person deposits, but it is the shipping center with one of the *lowest* customer service rankings, and by god if Anderson hasn't tried to get something, anything, out of the two twenty-two-year-old heroin addicts working the late shift the night before last, the ones who would've witnessed the drop-off.

'I'm about to head down there in person,' Anderson says, if Brian Castle would like to come along, to which Brian Castle replies, yep, he sure does.

The two men agree to meet there in under two hours, and this is how forces begin to collide. But you cannot know that forces are colliding as you are waving at cameras, as Toby Castle is waving, as you give Toby a kiss on the cheek and grin as wide as you ever have grinned, still waving, from the front stoop until you hear a high-pitched, near-primordial cry, and look beyond the cameras to the chubby black boy who, moments ago, was dangling upside down on the monkey bars but now, unstable for all his belly weight, has dropped, shoulder-first, to the ground.

The boy has landed sort of sideways. Like, *on his head*.

The photographers, they all rush to assist him, and seconds later they shout, 'Congressman Wilson! Bring him inside!' and now the heat is on for you to bring the dumb fat kid *into your house*.

You are a professional. Even though you are not generous, you are a professional, one who understands that one must always *appear* generous, and you have had to work extremely hard all your life to appear as generous, open-hearted as you do now, as the photographers lift the boy from the ground and carry him, Christ-like, up your front stoop. 'Geez, he isn't *bleeding* or anything,' slips out, but the reporters and paparazzi don't hear you, they are still flashing their bulbs at the boy as he's hauled through your green front door with the brass lion's-head knocker on live TV, straight into your living room and onto your canary-yellow velvet Victorian sofa, and Toby, she goes to the kitchen and runs a whole bunch of your expensive flour sacks right under the faucet as the boy is *writhing on your sofa,* howling in pain, and everyone's freaking out, tending to him like he's a wounded apostle, looking to see if the mother's outside, if anyone's with him, but the mother has let the boy play on the playground alone, and honestly, who even does *that* anymore?

'How old are you,' the reporters ask, snapping his picture.

The boy tells them 'ten.' He is ten years old.

'What is your name,' they ask, and he says his name's Elijah but everyone calls him 'Vicky,' because when he was three years old he ate an entire bottle of Vicks VapoRub.

'Owoo-woo!' Vicky howls, his neck, like, *really hurts,* and even though Vicky's the show, even though Toby

Castle has knelt down next to Vicky to apply the wet flour sacks as a makeshift cold compress, it is neither Toby Castle nor Vicky everyone's interested in; everyone is watching how you, Congressman Wilson, will interact with a wounded black child in your house. It's like: they know you'll be awkward, but *how* awkward, and for a moment all seems to have been forgotten about the aardvark, which is fine with you until Vicky sits up a little.

'Where's the *aardvark*,' he says.

He knows what an aardvark is, he says, because he learned about them in school. He is in fifth grade. He wants to see it, he says, and so this boy, you decide, the memory of your door being slammed in his face yesterday still fresh in his mind, is a cunning. Little. *Bastard*.

Vicky remembers everything. When the aardvark was delivered by FedEx, he says, and '*that man*' wouldn't let him see it (you, he is pointing at you), and suddenly the reporters are snapping photos of the boy sitting up on your sofa and pointing at you, and this looks bad, *real bad*, it's happening *live*, and you don't have the faintest clue what to do, how to get all of these people out of your house until, crossing the threshold, a six-foot-five-inch-tall black man fills the door, graceful as a horse, luggage in tow.

Enter Olioke.

'Everyone out!' shouts Olioke.

'Congressman Olioke!' the reporters cry with delight as he starts shoving them all out the door. 'Do you have a comment on the aardvark?' and Olioke, God Bless Olioke – from here on out, you promise yourself, no matter what, you will flat-out, hands-down *love* Olioke – doesn't even look at them as he calmly replies:

'I most certainly do *not*.'

With that, your townhouse is all at once empty except for you, Toby, Olioke, and the bastard child Vicky, who has not moved from your sofa and is now meekly requesting potato chips.

'I'll take care of him,' Toby says as Olioke puts down his luggage.

'Where is it,' he asks, and you lead Olioke downstairs, into the garage. You unlock the rear of the Tahoe.

You show him what occupies the trunk, the back seat.

Olioke looks at the aardvark. He is calm, and everything Olioke does is always very calm, he speaks plain and clear, never interjects, nor uses slang, nor even conjunctions, and you must admit that you feel better with Olioke standing next to you than you have in twenty-four hours, ever since the aardvark arrived at your front door.

'Possession of this aardvark,' he says, 'puts you in danger of breaking federal law because it was illegally poached,' and goes on to explain how he saw the aardvark on TV and knows all about it, it's why he called your landline – it was *safer* – and it's then that you realize *Olioke's* voice, that was the voice on the phone!

'That was you on the phone!' you say.

'You have to get rid of it,' he says, and calmly, slowly, tells you once more about the Herero and the Namaqua: how it all started after the German Emperor Wilhelm II took over from Otto von Bismarck, and how the kaiser, not a man known for his patience or tact, and against the counsel of his ministers, invaded South West Africa, plundered her resources, then dispatched Heinrich Göring and the criminal General Lothar von Trotha, who first attempted to colonize and then, after a revolt, savagely murdered Olioke's people, and it was more than *a hundred thousand souls*, and Olioke's own great-grandparents were actually *survivors* of the genocide –

This is all news to you. Because despite the fact that you share your townhouse with Rutledge and Olioke when Congress is in session, and you often hear them downstairs playing Parcheesi and eating peanut butter sandwiches, laughing in their cheap suits over lite beers in your kitchen, you have never once joined them, and you have spoken very little with Rutledge or Olioke in the six months that you've shared your townhouse (something you would *never* have done if you hadn't been pressured to do so from higher-ups, to curry favor), and all you know about Rutledge is that he's a Democrat from New Hampshire who works out a lot (he benches 280), and he has a wife and five sons whom he goes to see on some farm every weekend – and all you know about Olioke is that he's a Republican from Rhode Island who shops at Goodwill, that he has a wife and five daughters and he, too, takes off every weekend to see them at some crappy cottage by some crappy lake, and that he is black – African American – but you never knew that he was actually *from-Africa* African American, and up to this moment you have allowed little room in your consciousness for Africa, but now it feels as though Africa, it is all around you, and you can't help but freak out a little bit that Greg Tampico's foundation, *it* was in Namibia while Olioke is Namibian, as he spells it all out:

'It is commonly known,' Olioke says (and this is seriously how the man talks), 'that Heinrich Göring brought a stuffed aardvark to Africa sometime in the late eighteen hundreds.' It is also 'commonly known,' he continues, that Göring and the Germans *murdered people,* set in motion the horror that would follow vis-à-vis Von Trotha, who expelled Olioke's people from their own land, trapped them in the desert, and gave them no water. Or poisoned it.

'The Germans,' Olioke explains, 'they established "work camps" in South West Africa that were tested "effective"; camps that would,' he goes on to say, 'not long after, serve as models for Hitler,' and over the course of three years the Germans murdered more than ninety thousand Herero and more than ten thousand Namaqua, and this aardvark, Olioke says, is a totem of his country's brutalized past.

He lifts the aardvark by the base. Underneath, in one corner, engraved deep into the wood, is a little geometrical figure, a hooked cross, and you do not need confirmation from Olioke to understand what it is.

'So you're afraid of it,' you say, and Olioke smiles sympathetically at you, like you can't help that you're dumb.

'To the contrary,' he says. 'The Herero believe that the way against oppression is to wear the skins of the enemy. By wearing the skins of the enemy, the power of the oppressor is diminished, reappropriated.'

You smirk a little when Olioke tells you this. You can't help yourself. You've never really been comfortable when it comes to serious stuff like *oppression,* like *genocide,* and despite the fact that you have every reason to believe Olioke, the notion that some, like, random *tribe in Namibia* knows about the gigantic taxidermied blue-eyed aardvark currently lodged in the back of your Chevy Tahoe in the garage of Asher Place Townhouses in Foggy Bottom tickles you, gives you the giggles, and that's when Olioke, well versed in your immaturity and that of Your People, whips out his phone.

He shows you a picture of a group of modern Herero, costumed in what appear to be ridiculous Victorian outfits.

'The Herero are *very serious* about wearing the enemy,' Olioke says, and look at the men, he says, even today dressed in the costumes of their oppressors, as German cadets, and look at the women dressed in blooming Victorian dresses sewn from African fabrics, replete with puffed sleeves and bodices – and as you look at the costumes of the Herero, the image reminds you instantly of Ronald Reagan, of the vast collection of clothes imitating the former president that you've amassed in your closet upstairs, which no one on Earth has ever seen in full:

You have Reagan's same wide silk ties. His shiny tie pins. His silk handkerchiefs. You have his gold silk formal vest, his loafers, black and gleaming, several of his oxfords with the signature French cuffs, his V-neck cashmere sweaters, his sky-blue pajamas and, of course, his Bill Blass bathrobe, your personal favorite. In your closet also hangs Ronald Reagan's long black woolen coat, which you wear in winter. You wear his tan raincoat for everyday. His silk scarves are the color of ejaculate – you wear those too – and although you've never ridden a horse in your life, you also have the same pale blue cowboy shirt that Reagan wore, the same straw cowboy hat, and it is all a growing assemblage of items awaiting the day when you buy the 688-acre ranch in Virginia that you are one day hoping to buy that reminds you of Rancho del Cielo, Reagan's 688-acre 'Heaven's Ranch' in Santa Barbara, and you wonder who has it backward, you or the Herero: should a person wear the clothes of their enemy or the clothes of their hero?

One word Olioke used makes you worry that you might be in the wrong. That word is 'skins.'

You have always thought that by dressing like Ronald Reagan you would sort of, like, *become* Ronald Reagan, but standing here in your garage in your Calvin Klein silk trousers, your pink gingham button-down, you suddenly feel pathetic. Plastic. The cheap, dime-store version of Ronald Reagan, and the Gipper, he would *never* have worn what you're wearing – looking at Ronald Reagan, an elder statesman once wistfully told you, was like looking at a tree in autumn – and Olioke, his expression is like *he knows this already*, like he knows more about you than you know yourself, but let's face it, if you were to start wearing the skins of your enemy, you would have to begin with a damned marigold pantsuit.

Ladies and gentlemen, that will *never happen*.

You will make your peace with this. After all, you are not African. Olioke has 'a people' while you have a Favorability Rating, one which has, in all likelihood, nose-dived in one day. All you have is *Plaine Truth,* a missive cynically born from polled statistics. You have your plan to marry Toby Castle, to nihilistically seed her womb, to use Toby Castle to change your platform from Bachelor to Family Man, which might give Nancy Fucking Beavers a fucking run for her money, but the blue-eyed aardvark is still sitting in the back of your Tahoe and now, more than ever, it appears to be mocking you, and so it's time, you decide, at last, finally, to do something about the fucking aardvark.

'Toby!' you shout, and spring back upstairs to the living room.

Vicky's still lying on the couch, a happy little villain munching some Lay's which Toby somehow procured, but Toby, her face is changed, she's on the phone with her father, she says, a finger to her lips, and when she's finished, she looks at you, pale.

'Who is Greg Tampico,' she asks and shows you her phone.

On Toby Castle's phone is a photograph of a hand-some white man, young and fit, a shock of blond hair winging over his forehead, standing with a group of hand-some African people dressed in Victorian costumes, those whom you now know to be the Herero.

They are somewhere in Namibia. Greg Tampico's hands are resting on the shoulders of their little children, and on his face sits a wide, dumb smile.

You can't understand it. Tampico doesn't look blue at all. He looks happy, genuinely goddamn *happy*, far happier than *you* have ever been in your life, and there, front and center, is the gift the Herero are giving to

Greg Tampico: a gigantic taxidermied and professionally mounted aardvark.

There is no question that this is your aardvark. And you do not know how it made it from Hermann Göring's crazy Prussian hunting lodge all the way back to Namibia, but it did, because the Herero in the photo, they are gifting the aardvark to Tampico in gratitude for giving medical aid to their children for so many years, and it's a very important gift, loaded with meaning, and while Toby starts pummeling you with questions about your relationship, how *exactly* you know Greg Tampico, one of the biggest homos, *everyone* knows, in DC, the sadness you feel over losing him begins rising. Like, *you just did not expect to feel this way* but you do, and it's what writers for centuries have called 'melancholia' but because you don't read books, your language is limited; you cannot articulate the feeling you feel beyond the word 'sad': you are, like, all at once very *sad* that Tampico's dead, very *sad* that you will never again lie with him on the large zebra skin in the walk-up on King Street, and you are wondering if you will ever again laugh as freely and naturally as you laughed when Tampico would playfully take your pants zipper in his teeth, scratch his prickly chin on the soft of your belly, when Vicky puts down his potato chips and points at Toby's phone.

'That man is funny,' he says.

Toby says, 'Shush, your mom's on her way,' but you say to wait. Let him finish.

Vicky is ten years old. He lies only about homework and food, and he has seen the man on her phone before, he insists, yesterday, next to the playground across the street from Asher Place Townhouses, and the man was *funny*, Vicky says.

How funny, you say.

Vicky shrugs. 'I don't know, *funny*,' he says, and giggles as he tells the two congressmen and the blond lady about how he watched that man sitting in the front of a FedEx truck putting on a big fake beard and, Vicky says, like, these *really funny*. Thick. Eyeglasses.

∽

The death mask, it looks *divine*, Downing thinks the next morning as he preens the aardvark for Viewing. She is *ready, glowing*, the way her eyelids embrace Ostlet's blue-and-white eyeballs, and at the base are small sacks of skin which hang like little hammocks, the lightest of touches which gives the countenance, Downing correctly intuits, of love.

This is the beauty the taxidermist has sought: the aardvark, at first glance a veritable mess of biology, because it has been perfectly re-created in its natural state, mid-hunt, as though striking a mound of sand with one claw, its back arched profoundly, its head low with its ears raised, alert; and because Downing, it must be said, *loves Ostlet,* and the way he's worked the eyeballs reflect this, the aardvark demonstrates a look of confidence, of loving itself despite what it looks like to others, and there is also a bit of bravery in the *jiva,* the kind born only from the humility that comes from true wisdom and which avails itself to the aged of any living species, and it is exactly how Titus Downing, himself aged forty-one years to the day, gazed at his blind lover last night.

They lay together beneath the aubergine velvet drapes on his bed. Richard could no longer see him. But Titus awakened his memory of sight.

'Dickie,' he sighed, and tickled his fingertips on Richard's sternocleidomastoid. He pressed the side of his face against Richard's warm, round pectoralis major, sliding over the sternum, and he stuck his long, pointy nose into his lover's umbilicus, kissed the soft fur-mound of gray pubis before taking the prepuce in his mouth and holding between his lips the floppy glans, the subcutaneous fascia, and as Richard moaned with pure pleasure, Titus Downing's appetite blossomed. Afterward, he said he was *starving,* and Richard said to 'get up, get dressed,' and allowed Titus to lead him downstairs, into the kitchen, where, already accustomed to cooking half-blind, he assembled from what vegetables remained in Downing's pantry a light summery stew of onions, runner beans and marrow, and it was the first time since his childhood in Northumberland that someone who loved him had made food for Downing.

As the two men ate, they stood side by side, elbows linked, and Downing knew at once that this was, must be, what so many others called 'happiness' –

So it is that the taxidermist wanders around his shop on the morning of the Viewing in a happy stupor. The time, it is nigh, the aardvark is complete, he thinks, the shop is prepared, until a knock comes at the door and enter Downing's old roommate, noted prosthetic specialist Harold Skinner, who has arrived from London wearing the same tidy handlebar mustache he's always worn, and who will act as the bid-taker.

Following him, enter the theater troupe, and they are six boys wearing pink-and-yellow hose, papier-mâché rabbit ears on their heads, papier-mâché claws on their hands and feet, and the costumes don't look a *bit* like the costumes Downing has drawn; the boys, who have arrived two hours too early and half drunk, haven't taken it seriously and their long-snouted masks appear slipshod enough to be vaguely indecent.

Downing sends them outside to sober up, to practice, and the troupe does so laughing, making *oinking* sounds, extemporaneously spanking one another – and it is because of his exceedingly good mood this morning that Downing only *fleetingly* doubts whether the troupe really is up to snuff; whether these silly faux aardvarks might *actually* disrupt the particular mood of the *actual* aardvark, which Downing has set up in the center of his shop for the Viewing at precisely two o'clock, carefully positioned in the long beam of natural British sunlight which Downing well knows will appear.

In fact, over the next two hours, as the line of people begins to form outside underneath the twelve heads of stuffed stags, Downing's mind, it is elsewhere: upstairs, with his blind lover who waits for him naked on the bed, lying face-down because it feels good on his eyes, slowly wrapping a fresh bandage around his eye sockets, which he had agreed to show Downing last night.

Downing had lit a candle and held it up to Ostlet's face, which otherwise looked the same: there was his boxy hunter's jaw, his nubby boy's nose, his cheeks fat and round as ladies' pincushions, but above which, in the flickering light, sat two new ghoulish vacancies, shocking in both size and color and reminding Downing at once of a moss-coated cave he used to explore as a child in Northumberland.

The cave, wet and dark, was in Pauperhaugh, found only by traveling the length of the riverbank away from his farm, into the woods, and resembled a boulder with its middle scooped out. Late one afternoon, after his chores were finished, the boy Titus had decided to hide there, as was his wont, with a book until dinner. He cleared moss from the mouth and crawled inside, but as he, candlelit, began reading, he sensed that he was not alone, he heard breathing, and the boy could not see it but suspected it was Animal as it smelled muddy-sweet, and when he lifted his light and peered into the darkness, the outline of a small girl appeared, mud-covered and squatting.

She was naked, her legs wrapped up in her arms, and she grinned strangely at Titus, as though she had never done it before. Then she blew out his light!

The last thing he saw was her hair, which looked like a bird's nest had been glued to her head.

Titus, himself no dandy in his farm clothes, his little work boots, felt afraid in the darkness. Cold air chilled his legs. When he reached out a hand to make for the exit, the girl leaned forward, opened her wide, blackened maw, and she *bit* him. She got his right hand and did not let go, and it was a very deep bite between knuckles that drew blood – the uneven scar remains, though pale, on the taxidermist's hand even today – and after she tasted blood she began to whimper, a whimper which set her off into a long, inhuman howl, and young Downing had never heard such a thing, like an animal trapped in human skin, and as he fled the cave, never to return, the boy's ears rang, he felt a new, ripping pain in his hand, and it was one he would feel, on occasion, for years:

When he would finally leave Northumberland for Oxford; when he would awake at Oxford, finals looming, screaming out to Harold Skinner in the night; when he attended the Great Exhibition at Hyde Park, listening to Mr Darwin explain the new art called 'taxidermy,' a term, Darwin explained, for a beast's 'arrangement of skin.'

Once Downing set up his own taxidermy shop in Leamington Spa and arranged the twelve heads of adult stags outside his front door, he felt safer. He believed he had forgotten about the girl, but at the same time he did not really forget; she had simply moved from his hand to his heart, and if there is a secret to the talent of Titus Downing, it must be this: the girl is with him whenever he subjugates himself to his craft, looking for the raw, Animal feeling that will help him to re-create the *jiva*. She lives *in* him, and as he stared into Richard's dark, carcass-colored eye sockets last night, Downing surprised himself when they resembled two great, gaping mouths and the girl returned to him once more – her black, open mouth, the cave's moss-scent, the wet air chilling his legs – the old pain seized his right hand and so she, too, must be partly to blame for why the taxidermist cares so little about the drunk boys in the theater troupe who are, at this moment, belting out a tune they've just invented called 'Cocks and Fox.'

'Get to work, aardvarks!' he shouts as more people arrive, and the boys start to prance in a frenzy, crouching down on all fours, throwing their snouts about on the cobblestones, looking nothing like aardvarks as the crowd bifurcates, forming two long lines, each beginning at the front door of 24 Victoria Terrace, at the intersection of Bath Street and the Terrace Leam.

∽

It's begun, which means that it's over. Upstairs, the TV is shouting something about a photograph that's *just been procured*, and CONGRESSMAN ALEXANDER PAINE WILSON OWNS A NAZI AARDVARK, and you don't have to look at the television to know that Hermann Göring's hunting lodge photo, the one with the aardvark, is everywhere, so you look at your phone where there are now 5063 unread text messages and 8292 unread emails, and you do not need to look further to know your Favorability Rating's kaput.

'Toby,' you say. 'Toby, listen.'

'How do *you* know Greg Tampico,' she demands again, and you almost tell her, but don't –

Because you still don't know if Vicky *actually saw* Greg Tampico yesterday morning in the FedEx truck, if it was *actually* Tampico putting on a disguise, and frankly, it just doesn't sound like him because Tampico was ser-iously, like, *so insanely bad* at keeping the lid on surprises. Like, this one time he planned to surprise you on your birthday with jet-skiing on the Potomac but couldn't hold it past breakfast, so if it was *actually* Tampico delivering the aardvark, you think, he would have been quick, at least quicker than this, to laugh at the joke, he would have at least *texted* or something by now, he would have sought out and downloaded a stupid *aardvark emoji*, which is why as you start mumbling banalities at Toby to let your memory function, returning to the hot, front stoop of 2486 Asher Place yesterday morning when nothing was working, you remain unconvinced, recalling only that the deliveryman's beard was certainly odd-looking, the eye-glasses were certainly thick, and the general physique of the deliveryman could only *maybe* pass for Greg Tampico's, but who knows, you can't say for certain, and you do not worry what it says about you either if you did or did not recognize him.

You have *no idea* why Toby's father, Brian Castle, would send Toby the picture of Greg Tampico, you explain. All you can say is you know the guy from some fundraiser, and yeah, you guess clumsily, the aardvark *could* be from him but you don't know for sure, and this you, like, *totally swear* as Vicky's mother, slender and pretty, arrives at the door.

Vicky's mother does not knock when she enters. Nor does she look at you, let alone thank you. She looks at *Olioke* and thanks *him* – for what, you have no idea – and the way Vicky's pretty mother ignores you and goes right for Olioke makes you feel, in some despicable way, on the defensive. And Toby Castle is saying, 'This isn't right,' and, 'Something's not right,' but Olioke, God Bless Olioke, he has said zilch so far to Toby about the Herero, about what he knows of Greg Tampico, so while he's dealing with Vicky's mother you shoot Olioke some gratitude, like, *thanks, bruh,* but he just stares at you. Blank. Behind the blank look is a glimmer of innocence. It's *willful,* like the man is deliberately hiding something about which he needs to appear innocent, and that's when it comes at you, in a slither:

Olioke is leaking pictures to the media. He could have done the last one just moments ago, walking up behind you, from the garage. Because who else other than *Olioke* knows about the hunting lodge? Who else knows the aardvark's whole history, would have *known* all about that fucking photo of Tampico being gifted the aardvark in Namibia – but why, *why* would Olioke throw you under the bus like this, you wonder, and tell Toby to *wait, just fucking wait,* you'll explain about Greg Tampico if she'll wait, but she doesn't believe you. She's through.

'This is over,' she says, and, 'I hope everything works out for you, Alex.'

Toby stands up straight, and her posture is perfect, like she's already forgotten about you and is ready to meet Someone New.

Exit Toby Castle, striding out the front door with no thought of you or your clothes that she's wearing, and she is closely followed by Vicky and his pretty mother, yanking him down the front steps, Vicky howling the entire way out, 'The *aardvark,* I want to see the *aardvark!*' until the front door closes and the sound of a thousand flicking shutters explodes from the cameras of the reporters, the paparazzi, who now, it appears, occupy the whole block.

You turn around and face Olioke. 'Did you leak that goddamned Nazi photograph?' you ask him.

Olioke says nothing. He goes into your kitchen and takes out the peanut butter. He starts looking around for his rust-dotted paring knife.

'Where is my knife?' he says.

'Fuck your knife,' you say, and stomp upstairs to your bedroom in a manner you haven't re-created since you were thirteen.

You sit down on your mattress.

Your mattress is a ten-layered, California King-sized Kluft Palais Royale ($32878) made with ten pounds of cashmere, of mohair, silk and wool, and pressing both hands flat upon it, you steel yourself, then grab the remote and turn on your Samsung to watch the charges which have been leveled against you:

You have probably broken the Lacey Act. You are probably a Nazi sympathizer. You are (or were) engaged to Toby Castle whose father, Brian Castle, got rich by inventing a business to help tech companies hemorrhage U.S. jobs overseas.

A photograph of Vicky from just, like, *seven minutes ago* in your living room appears on the screen.

It is not your purported kindness toward Vicky that anyone cares about; they only care about the canary-yellow velvet Victorian sofa upon which the young Vicky lies. For apparently, although you paid only $1900 for it, it's worth *well over twelve thousand,* and *what junior congressman,* Nancy Fucking Beavers is asking right now on MSNBC, can afford such a luxury?

So despite the fact that in your three years in Congress you've passed more legislation than any other Republican freshman, secured $55 million in funding for Virginia, have been called a 'hard worker,' a 'rising star' by the House Speaker, and despite the fact that you've appeared on *Fallon* to talk about your workout regime, even found yourself on a list of 'Hottest Congressmen' on BuzzFeed, add another charge to the pile: an investigation's begun. A watchdog group has been formed to *dig into your finances,* and when they dig deep enough, which they most certainly will, they will unearth a veritable buffet of improprieties, all of which true: you *did* sell your parents' house, the house you grew up in, to a major Republican donor for much more than it was worth to buy a fancy-ass Victorian townhouse in Foggy Bottom, and you *have* charged an unpardonable several hundreds of thousands on private flights, on lavish oak furniture for office and home, to the taxpayer, and it's hard to explain *why* but you just feel somehow *owed,* like you are just taking money from America like a child would from a parent who gave them no love, and Tampico's aardvark will fade into the background as, in the coming weeks, a congressional committee will form, the IRS will seize your accounts, and a group of men dressed in, like, *black jumpsuits or something* will arrive at 2486 Asher Place holding several cardboard boxes far bigger than the aardvark's box, march upstairs to your closet, and pack up and haul away your entire collection of clothes just like the clothes Ronald Reagan was wearing in *Images of Greatness*.

Sitting alone on your Kluft Palais Royale, the scent of Toby Castle's vagina still mushrooming your bedsheets, it hardly matters now how accomplished you've been. What you've done. There will be no airports. And although the name 'Alexander Paine Wilson' will be forever etched somewhere in the backed-up anus of history, there will be no legacy of yours at all except this media blip, which, six months from now, no one will recall because everything happened before anything happened.

You look at your phone, where you have 9491 unread text messages and 12722 unread emails. You enter *aardvark* into the search function.

It appears over ten thousand times.

You enter *tampico*.

There is nothing from Greg Tampico. All that comes up is a news article sent to you early yesterday morning from your assistant, Barb Newberg.

Barb Newberg knows you like Ronald Reagan and, out of kindness or boredom, has sent you an article about Reagan's birthplace, which is a modest two-bedroom apartment in a modest two-story brick building currently housing a First National Bank, sandwiched between an insurance company and a funeral parlor in the tiny village of Tampico, Illinois.

Thought you would enjoy this – Barb ☺, she wrote.

It is not the bizarre coincidence of the two Tampicos which interests you, nor is it the building itself. It's the unassuming funeral parlor next door which reminds you that today, Monday, is the funeral.

Murphy & Milliken's Funeral Home in Alexandria, you remember, at two o'clock sharp, and the place is on Prince Street, which is not far at all from Greg Tampico's walk-up on King Street – and you will go to the funeral because you still could be wrong; if the boy Vicky indeed saw the man as he says he did, then Tampico is alive, just being unusually withholding, just pissed off about the last time you saw each other and is, like, *just totally fucking with you* – and if that is true, you are wondering, then what on God's Green Earth, as your mother would say, will be in the coffin?

3

E NTER TWELVE GENTLEMEN IN gray and black broad-
cloth, their silk neckties flash with color. Enter the
lawyers and bankers and schoolteachers, the civil engi-
neers and physicians; enter the journalists, newspapermen
in their bowler hats like the kind street monkeys wear
until enter Walter Potter, Downing's chief competitor, and
Walter Potter is ginger-blond, bow-tied and mutton-
chopped, and there can be no doubt that it's Potter
because a few people have spotted him, asked for his
autograph, and the newspapermen are writing everything
down, *interviewing Potter* on the street outside Downing's
Viewing, the taxidermist peevishly notices, until Potter
tells them he's there because, like everyone else, he's curious to see the African Aardvark and he's been a longtime
admirer of Downing's, and he promises them that this will
indeed be a Big Viewing, and it turns out, to start, that
Walter Potter is right:

The event is free. As the minutes tick by and all

Gentlemen have arrived, enter the men from the unskilled professions, these miners, textile mill workers, railway porters all sporting rolled trousers, country tweeds, their boots filthy with coal, and from there, in ratty cotton jackets with badly stitched seams, enter the costermongers, appearing for once in public without their rickety vegetable carts; enter the butty-gangs of sewer men, the stench of the toshers and ratcatchers until enter the coal-faced sweepers of both street and chimney, and the men mingle harmoniously, each finding his own kind, the sun is out, it is a very hot day, it is August, and everyone's watching the gay-drunk boys in the theater troupe tossing their fake snouts, scratching the cobblestones with their fake claws, pointing, laughing, as the peaked wooden doors of the All Saints Church across the street bust open and out spill the fat clergymen, rosy-hot in their cassocks – they are leaving the cool vestibule of the church to come View the aardvark – and Downing can sense that it is, at last, finally Time.

'*Enter*,' he says, and that is all as the first Viewers walk into the shop, see the aardvark, and gasp.

From here on out, Downing will step aside. Because Downing, he never stays for his Viewings. He always leaves the shop and goes to a pub, The Green Otter, for a pint while the critics evaluate the work he's accomplished, and this is because he already knows what he's done, he knows that it's all he could do, and this afternoon is no different as Downing nods soberly to Harold Skinner, who, just one year ago, took bids on the African giraffe, selling it for a very high price to the New Walk Museum – this afternoon, leaving his shop, Downing happily gives Skinner the proverbial reins and walks without consternation or care past All Saints.

He strolls down Bath Street, hangs a left onto Clarence Street and takes the curved side alley which leads to The Green Otter, where he will spoil himself and Richard tonight with dinner in a takeaway basket. And the taxidermist does not hold back when offered the orange duck and sweet peas or the beans with fried bacon, he orders both, as the hunger which appeared the night before has not abated, and when he orders two full bottles of a decent claret, he samples it slowly, like nothing else is going on in the world, and only *then*, for *himself, now,* does he get his pint.

Downing always orders one single pint, tall and frothy, to celebrate the completion of any stuffed beast, and this afternoon, sun melting off the pub's little round windows all made from crown glass, he sits alone in a corner, sipping, the sweet hops coats his tongue, slides down his throat in a warm, pleasing tickle, and as he drinks, his mind utterly clears: he is thinking about nothing. He longs for nothing.

His soul is neither attached to the past nor diverted to the future, and he's not thinking about Richard, nor the aardvark, nor is he thinking of the people in or not in attendance at the Viewing, and he is not even thinking of the arrival of the young Rebecca Ostlet, nor the cost of this extravagant dinner – all of which he might have behooved to think about had he known what was about to take place in his absence.

∽

You hate going to funerals, always have. You don't like to think about dead things, or even sick things, and for the better part of your education at UVA, the professors all seemed to push *death* and *relativity* and *history* at you, and you preferred then, and still prefer now, to think about *life* and *certainty,* you prefer to forget the past to embrace the future, but no one ever talked about those things, and you often wonder why everyone in college was always trying to be so admirably pessimistic when you're so admirably optimistic, and it's this sort of optimistic thought, the one that Greg Tampico might be alive, consequences be damned, that propels you off your mattress, out of your bedroom, downstairs, away from the kitchen where Olioke sits eating his fucking sandwich (you, like, *seriously flat-out hate Olioke*) – and once more into the garage, into the Tahoe, where your departure from 2486 Asher Place is remarkably swift.

Your departure is swift because no one expects it. The photographers are stunned when the garage doors lift and the Tahoe is suddenly borne out into sunlight. They barely have time to turn on their cameras, rush their white vans, before you're off, and now all of America's watching your Tahoe on TV, OJ-like, as you hurtle toward Alexandria.

You have to lose them. You understand that you have to lose them as you maniacally zoom through the stoplights, peeling left and right all over DC, but the paparazzi are good, they must take, like, *driving lessons* or something, and someone's even called the police, because sirens: in the distance, you hear them coming and they are coming for *you,* and holy hell, could this look *worse*?

This is it, you are thinking, this is fucking *it,* you are fucking *fucked,* and so it goes for several minutes until, by god, a miracle:

When you turn onto Constitution Ave., enter the god-damn President of the United States and his motorcade.

You are not usually a fan of the president, a fifty-nine-year-old Democrat from Ohio who, in a recent cabinet meeting, personally praised Nancy Fucking Beavers for her tenacity over some minor family-leave legislation, which she somehow got passed as some bullshit thing called a 'citizen advocate' – but man oh man, are you a fan now: the president's collection of black Chevy Tahoes is crawling down Constitution like a parade of great beetles, and the white trucks of the paparazzi are, like, *totally blocked* by security, they are stopped right away by the cops on the street, but you? The cops wave you right by! And how *remarkably easy* is it for you to drive past them – in a gutsy move, you give them a wave – disappearing into the president's fleet, and just like that, you're invisible, you have managed to confuse everyone. It's like *no one can tell whose Tahoe is whose,* and you have absolutely zero compunction about pretending for one blissful moment that *you* are the president, which you do, because there are people outside, people on the side-walk, cheering and jeering, and in their hands they hold the requisite colorful signage, and it's all protesting the usual fare, none of it you read – but just as you break, hanging an unexpected sharp right onto the 9th Street Expressway, which will carry you around the Smithsonian, into a tunnel that *goes under the Mall,* you observe a little girl in pigtails sitting on the shoulders of her father.

She can't be more than five. High in the air, she holds a crude drawing she's made with her Crayolas, and though it's maybe obvious to no one but you, it's clearly an aardvark, a gigantic aardvark with a gigantic black swastika scrawled onto its belly – and this is the last thing you see before disappearing below ground, toward 395, and when you emerge from the darkness you are once more headed for the 14th Street Bridge, and when you at last cross it, the bridge over the Potomac, you do it alone.

You are unmoored, unencumbered. You cannot recall a time in your life when you've felt more relaxed, more at ease, and you even laugh a little bit as you reach for your Ray-Bans in the glove compartment and put them on only to, out of both habit and pleasure, catch a glimpse of yourself in the rearview.

There is no giant stuffed beast taking up the back of the Tahoe.

The aardvark is *gone*. And just like that, your easy feeling at once gives way to worry and doom. The relief that you expected to feel getting rid of the aardvark: it isn't there because *you* didn't do it. Someone, somehow, has, like, totally *gotten to her,* which means they were, like, *inside your car,* inside your *house* – and you feel pretty freaked out about this, if truth be told, like someone has vacuumed your insides. Without the aardvark, the Tahoe, it feels super huge, super empty, and you realize that you sort of *miss* her, the way she looked at you all *sad* and *coy,* like the way Greg Tampico always looked at you –

It's hard to explain. No one had ever looked at you like that before, likely will never again, but whatever happened to her, you can't go back now; you have no choice but to continue speeding toward Greg Tampico's funeral with nothing but a new faint light shining into the black cave of your heart: that this could all be some kind of joke. Or some accident.

You don't know whether Greg Tampico is dead or alive, whether Vicky actually saw Greg Tampico disguising himself *in* freaking *corpus,* or whether it was someone else putting on those big fake glasses, that beard, but if so, it is someone the likes of whom you cannot, or refuse to, imagine.

∽

The question of the immortality of animal souls is something Rebecca Ostlet has long considered. She rejects the Cartesian view of animals as insentient machines, and she dismisses Aristotle's position as arrogant: 'As nature makes nothing purposeless or in vain,' he said, 'all animals must have been made by nature for the sake of men,' and Rebecca, rather disgusted even by Darwin, who regularly differentiated between 'man' and the 'lower animals,' is impressed by no man who believes he is superior to the beasts, and Goethe too, she feels, was wrong: an animal is not 'an end in itself' but a sensitive, knowing, godly creature and therefore, just like man, animals must *sail,* she believes, *with immortal souls,* and the impression was made early upon her after reading *Agnes Grey,* Anne Brontë's first novel, published in 1847, the year twenty-eight-year-old Rebecca Green was born.

She was appalled by a single phrase spoken by the cruel Mrs Bloomfield: 'the creatures were all created for our convenience,' Bloomfield said, and Rebecca found the word 'convenience' so abhorrent in that application that the young woman promptly discontinued her study of medicine at the University of Edinburgh, where she had entered in 1871, just two years after the first seven women gained entry, and, despite initial protests from the male faculty, was eventually granted permission to transfer her coursework to botany.

Rebecca had taken one course, however, from Sir Richard Ostlet, which she enjoyed. The course was called 'Practical Mammalogy,' in which Sir Richard regularly championed the existence of the souls of beasts, often quoting Liebniz's 'A New System of Nature' from way back in 1695, which argued that animals are *self-organized*, they are not 'matter which comes to be organized,' and Hieronymus Rorarius, a Hungarian papal diplomat who wrote even earlier, in 1547, that 'brutes frequently make better use of their reason than men,' and Rebecca found herself so fascinated by the man Ostlet, who advocated as such for animals, who traveled the world to study mammals in their natural habitats, that she entered his dark office one bright morning and delivered, in a flat, pragmatic tone, a brief treaty explaining why Rebecca Green and Sir Richard Ostlet should marry.

Richard's eyes had widened as she spoke, they grew dazzlingly *bulbous*, but the young woman was not deterred; in fact, she was amused when he coughed and apologized, said that his eyes always *bulged* like that, and he agreed that marrying made good sense – that is, if she could put up with his bad eyes, and with what would most certainly become his eventual blindness.

'I do not mind one bit,' Rebecca said.

They married the following spring. For the occasion, Rebecca wore a blue long-sleeved muslin, a little orange hat with a cluster of matching orange pelargonium from the Palm House in Kew Gardens adorning one side, and that evening, Richard, in preparation for a months-long journey to the Galapagos, showed her their new flat, which he purchased for her as a wedding gift, on Gloucester Walk in London, and, expecting that she would be lonely without him for these many months, Ostlet also presented his new wife with three wriggling, rust-colored puppies, each one a female purebred Irish setter with smooth, long-haired ears, conical heads, and Rebecca, in honor of *Agnes Grey*, named them Anne, Charlotte, and Emily – and so it is with the Brontës in tow that Rebecca Ostlet's carriage drops her off at 24 Victoria Terrace in Royal Leamington Spa to View the aardvark, her husband's final work.

The dogs, fully grown, spill out of the carriage in a trail of excited fire.

Rebecca alights, takes one glance at the two long lines which have formed at Titus Downing's taxidermy shop, and instantly observes that while there appear to be men of every British stripe, she is the only woman, at least from where she stands, in attendance.

At first, this hardly fazes Rebecca Ostlet. As a woman in science, she's used to it, and she nods to Gentlemen and Lowlifes alike when they tip their hats, yet it is only when the theater troupe spies her in her new cuirass bodice, masculine jacket, and necktie – it's the latest fashion in London, a dress which is extremely tight fitting, long-waisted and long-boned with the worst kind of corset all the way down to the hips, a drawn-back polonaise that ruches in peacock, over her rear – that she learns the reason, what has kept the women away: the drunk boys see Lady Ostlet in her new garb and whinny their pig heads. Long rabbity ears flap their cheeks.

Their papier-mâché claws air-dance as she walks closer, and when she stops to watch them, they pretend to hump one another as they blow into a popular John William Hobbs tune, a little chorus that is meant to be sung softly, gently, so as to create *irony,* but the boys eschew irony for vulgarity and belt it out loud at Rebecca in a surprisingly taut six-part harmony:

> *Phyllis is my only joy,*
> *Faithless as the winds and seas;*
> *Sometimes forward, sometimes coy,*
> *Yet she never fails to please,*
> *Yet she never fails to please.*

The Brontës, confused by the dancing aardvarks, start barking and move, long-legged, round the troupe, whining at their humping with glistening eyes, waffing the boys' legs with their feather-tails, but Rebecca Ostlet barely registers the boys as she walks through them, ignoring the way they rub their floppy snouts on her bustle and train, oinking *Phyllis! Phyllis!* like idiot pigs as she lifts it.

She steps one of her small woman-feet onto Titus Downing's doorstep, under the stag heads, then the other, and enters the taxidermy shop.

The man himself is in absentia. Rebecca genially skims Downing's stuffed geese and stuffed pheasants, his ducks and dogs, all his stuffed fish and stuffed rabbits, a collection of foxes, and is particularly taken with a shiny taupe vixen with an elegant, upturned snout that stands in the center of Downing's shopwindow.

The tods have been arranged so they appear to protect her, and the arrangement, Rebecca thinks, is absurd. The vixen, known for her cunning, is perfectly capable of taking care of herself and her brood, she needs not the protection of the rather skittish-looking tods – pray, the way Downing has them arranged, it rather looks like an *ambush,* she thinks – and while the shop fills and refills with Gentlemen all quickly moving past the other taxidermied creatures to make for the aardvark, Rebecca Ostlet, alone with the vixen, puts her hand on its soft head, admiring the look on its face, the eyes half-slanted and competent, as though she has been recently nursing.

Rebecca can count on one hand the number of times she and Richard actually completed the act of love.

'I am so much *older,* darling,' he would explain when they lay together, or it was difficult for him to quiet his mind from his work, he would say, and he understood if she was disappointed in him, and had to confess that he did not know what she needed but explained that he, for one, needed *rather little*, which is why the grief she experienced when she learned of his death was compounded.

For although Richard had left her a sizeable income, more than enough to last for a lifetime, it was appearing likely that she, closing fast in on thirty, would not have a child. And how many wasted, lonely months had she spent on Gloucester Walk, walking her dogs in the parks, either Holland or Hyde, waiting for Richard to return from his trips, and each time he returned, she could usually get just one night out of him before he fell back into diffidence, self-pity, and it was a peculiar, melancholic side of him that she did not expect when they married, as around everyone and everything else, the man was so abundantly *cheerful*, so *giving*, and it was less than a year into her new marriage that Rebecca realized her mistake.

As she lingers alone in Downing's shop amidst the woody scent of sweet cedar oils, of wet skin, fur and feathers, of salt of tartar, of palm wine, of chalky plasters, earth-and-water clays, of any number of preservative soaps and astringents, powders and lime, it is the recognition of the rosemary pine-musk of camphor, the familiar stink which always emanated from Richard, that at last gives Rebecca Ostlet the courage she needs to turn away from the vixen.

It is two o'clock. The sun pours relentless into Titus Downing's shop, casting onto the face of the aardvark a wide and clean arm of new light.

The face, she finds, whiskered all the way down the snout, is soft, its mien kindly looking, so similar to what she often sees in the Brontës after they've eaten their dinner. The aardvark's hide gleams yellow-pink at the top, brown at the bottom, and whispers of dark fur launch out from the back of the thick legs – plantigrade at the front, digitigrade at the back – in sharp contrast to the ears, so broad, so thin that the sunlight shines *through* them, instantly reminding Rebecca Ostlet of the peach-colored inner fold of a tremendous conch that Richard brought home for her from the Galapagos, and suddenly standing among the Gentlemen all silently Viewing the aardvark, Rebecca feels, for a moment, a brand-new kind of reverence. Her own gender washes out of her. She is not a woman among men but a human among humans, and imagines the Gentlemen feel the same way: it is a kind of collective prayer for this ridiculous creature with the ears of a rabbit, the snout of a pig, and with that one hoof-claw raised, it absolutely *does* look awake, alive, as though it might walk straight off its mount!

More, there is something *familiar* about the creature that Rebecca Ostlet has observed: something in the flat space of its forehead, she thinks, which is low and roomy, or perhaps in the way Downing has positioned the eyelids so they appear to hammock the eyes, and the kindness in the expression, she thinks, is a shock, it almost *looks human,* which is strikingly odd against the rolling, furry back arched up to bear the weight of its incredulous belly, so *round* – yet when she lifts one hand to stroke it, as she has done with the vixen, a Gentleman moos:

'Madam, I wouldn't do that.'

Twelve dark-suited men encircle the aardvark. Their hands are in their pockets. They have Viewed her not reverently but soberly, without generosity or even amusement.

'Don't touch it,' the man says. 'It's indecent.'

'*Vulgar,*' says another.

A third Gentleman nods. 'Quite right, John. Quite right.'

In turns, the aardvark is called by each man 'obscene.' It is 'an abomination,' like something discovered in some cave of some unholy world, but the men in their suits are not scientists, Rebecca remembers, they are just rich – they cannot love what they do not understand, and they only understand money – and as it is such a very hot day, outfitted as they are in formal wool suits, the men's cheeks flush, they grow testy, any mild discomfort, they believe, is a slight against their god-given status, so within the aardvark, they cannot see beauty; in fact, she seems to be *mocking* them as long beads of sweat slide down their temples, and Downing *really might have thought to provide refreshments,* Rebecca thinks, for his guests, for the people who have all come to stand in line in the hot sun to gaze upon an *Orycteropus afer* in early August in Leamington Spa. But there is nothing.

Outside, the young boys snort in their snouts while inside the grown men sweat and scowl. They feel bored, cheated, and the sun is now positively baking the room, and the Brontës, shaking their fur coats as though wishing to toss them from their bodies, begin idiotically barking at the door leading up to Downing's flat.

It is not long before everyone starts filing out.

The Gentlemen walk perhaps a bit too quickly away from Downing's shop, and when the others in line, from the Priests to the Sweepers, see the Gentlemen flee, when they see the men's faces, all pink and downcast, they, one by one, decide it's not worth it, it's too hot out, and away they go; the lines hugging the shop splinter, peel off, until only four people remain: Rebecca Ostlet, noted prosthetic specialist Harold Skinner, Walter Potter, and a corpulent German man with tiny hands, pouchy cheeks, and a wispy, mal-grown Imperial mustache that looks vaguely pubic.

'I'm Potter,' Walter Potter says, offering a hand to Harold Skinner. 'At last we meet.'

'I'm Skinner,' says Harold Skinner. 'Not Downing. If you would like to buy the aardvark, I'm here to take bids.'

Walter Potter regards Harold Skinner with surprise. 'Downing's not here?' he asks.

Skinner affirms that, no, he is not.

Walter Potter leans over the aardvark, inspecting Downing's craft, and Rebecca watches his hands move artfully over the pelage, feeling for seams, but Downing has worked the seams with a size 25 waxed needle, no bigger than a quilting pin, and Walter Potter, himself sporting a truly regal set of ginger-blond muttonchops, loudly breathes in and out over his mustache as he whispers, *'It's beautiful,'* and handles the aardvark's kangaroo tail like it's a great, caught fish. The legs are like trunks. 'It is *truly nature,'* he says, and moves his face to the face of the aardvark, at which point he stands up, startled.

He asks Rebecca and Skinner if they know what Downing did with the eyes.

In the sunlight of Titus Downing's taxidermy shop, Richard Ostlet's blue irises bulge.

'The eyeball can only be preserved in animals locally sourced,' Potter says, and goes on to inquire how Downing preserved the eyes from a creature from Africa. Was it immersion in Mueller's Fluid for three whole weeks? Or maybe some kind of humectant, made from isopropyl alcohol? Or were the eyes frozen solid in ice and salt until sliced into lateral halves, then placed into a chloral solution before being placed into a glycerin solution? Does anyone know?

Rebecca Ostlet looks closer. Wild mammals, as far as she knows, have brown eyes, and only human beings – or perhaps the rare dog or goat she has seen – have *blue* eyes, and blue eyes *do not occur in the wild,* she recalls from one of Richard's lectures as she realizes, with horror, what the pale, ghoulish taxidermist has done.

'Are you all right, madam,' Walter Potter asks, and he and Harold Skinner each take hold of one of Lady Ostlet's arms.

She sits herself down in a chair.

It is not the gruesome act of Downing having inserted her husband's shellacked eyeballs into the eye sockets of a gigantic stuffed aardvark that bothers Rebecca Ostlet; it is her certainty that the ghost of her husband is looking for them, is *still* looking for them, that it could be *nearby,* which is why she glances nervously out of the shop window, whispers faintly for the Brontës to come to her side, but the Brontës whine louder, scratching at the door leading upstairs to Downing's flat, and Rebecca suddenly struggles to breathe in the cuirass.

Potter and Skinner both look to the German man, malingering in the corner. 'Get water,' they say.

The German points at the aardvark. He knows all about them, he says, and has been to the south of Africa several times. He is about to go there again. Because Germany has a shot at a trade surplus. France now owns Algeria. Britain's at the Cape. Even Portugal's in Angola, Mozambique – but aardvarks, he says, do not have blue eyes, and points again. *'Blaue Augen,'* he says, perversely delighted, *this* aardvark has *blue eyes,* and it's the same delighted look that he, thirty-six-year-old Heinrich Göring, will in three years give nineteen-year-old Franziska Tiefenbrunn, the young Bavarian peasant with astonishing bright blue eyes that, when she looks at him in the moronic way she does, will remind him of the aardvark which is about to come into his possession; 'Fanny' Tiefenbrunn, soon to become Fanny Göring, will, halfway into their marriage, bear a fourth child, Hermann, who will inherit, to his father's equal delight, the same bright blue eyes of his mother.

'Are you sure you're all right,' Walter Potter says to Rebecca, and at that moment the Brontës, united in their cause, at long last manage to force open the door.

In a flying train of pink tongues, of rust-colored fur, the panting dogs tear up the staircase into Downing's flat. The staircase is narrow, the dogs fight into a line, making headlong for Downing's bedroom to reunite with their master, Sir Richard Ostlet, who is, as exactly no one could

have guessed, lying bare-assed and prostrate upon a canopied bed decorated only with lush velvet curtains the color
of aubergine.

∽

Murphy & Milliken's Funeral Home is a flat, one-story
brick building that looks like something that survived the
Eighties, but barely. It gets a 1.2 rating on Yelp. There is
a sad little roundabout in front of the joint, a place for the
Bereaved to pull up fancily in their cars, and the roof is
gray, broad, its overhang sort of too-big, trying lamely to
imitate the roof of a cozy thatched hut, and it's all remin-
iscent of those motels you've seen along rural highways,
like it's the sort of place that might be a place in the out-
skirts of Roanoke, Lynchburg, but here, in Alexandria,
the building has been forgotten, overshadowed by its
more industrious neighbors, which are two seven-story
parking garages, a long-abandoned stripe of the Metro,
and a Crate & Barrel outlet that takes up most of the
acreage and glows whitely behind the funeral parlor like
some kind of alien spacecraft.

You park your car in back. No one is here. No one is
here because according to your phone it's only 12:20 p.m.

The funeral won't begin for over an hour.

At the front door, there is no sign mentioning anything about a service today, there are no flowers that have
been delivered, there's no guest book to sign, and through
the building's windows, which are decorated with these
truly pall-looking purple faux-velvet drapes, the inside

looks dark and all this must be, you deduce, because you are early, which is why you're surprised, when you push the front door, that it opens.

The smell hits you first – it's a perfume you can't locate, floral or herbal or something – and the brown wall-to-wall, which is everywhere, just absorbs it. You cross the carpet and walk silently through an atrium, wondering how in the *hell* Greg Tampico ended up in a place like this when you thought he had money, and if not money then, like, at least, *taste*, and it occurs to you that you actually know next to nothing about Greg Tampico's friends or his family, nor even his coworkers from the Happiness Foundation, and maybe you don't know any of them because you never asked, maybe it was never important, or maybe too dangerous, or maybe because what you've known about Tampico, up to now, has always been enough for you:

Omnivore. He'll eat anything.
Laugh, when genuine, is embarrassingly
  high-pitched.
Underarms, when wet, develop meat-scent.
Smokes cigarettes on his back, with legs crossed.
His voice-lull in bed, like a radio on low.

You are inside for only a few minutes, wandering the parlor's gloomy, scented interior, before you appear in front of a shop of some kind, and you have never conceived that there would be an opportunity to *sell things* at a funeral home, but this is America. There's a counter, a register. They sell coffins.

You have never seen a real coffin before. Not one up close and in person, and there are four options for coffins ranging in price from $895 to $3995, which to you sounds pretty cheap. Each of the coffins on display is lined with shiny white silk that is not silk, it's *sateen,* padded with cotton, and some have frills, and all have lace or bows, enormous white pillows, and though they are made with hardwoods like cherry, walnut or mahogany, and are covered in so much polyurethane that they shine like new cars, and though you have never before thought seriously of your own death in your life, you make the decision, here and now, that when you die you will not go the *burial route,* you will go the *cremation route,* and you're apparently not alone in your thinking, for across from the coffins, a much more diverse selection of urns ranging from $95 to $495 are displayed, and it's clear that here's Murphy & Milliken's real business: selling urns.

The urns display nameplates like Trinity Sunset, Everlasting Symphony, Majestic Star – all but the smallest and cheapest urn, the one that looks made of aluminum and resembles an old-fashioned milk pail and is named, in an exercise of zero imagination, 'Infinity.' You pick it up, and the Infinity urn is lightweight, somehow weirdly *appealing,* and you glance around and consider stealing it when, from somewhere outside the store, a vacuum goes on.

You put back the urn. You exit the store. The vacuum is still going, but it's not close by, and just around the corner is a set of wide wooden doors, soundless when opened, which send you into what appears to be, at first glance, a small courtroom.

It's not a real courtroom. It's a courtroom like what you might see in a grade-school production of *Inherit the Wind,* and you should know since it's the only play in which you ever took part. There are church pews, six on a side, and the twelve pews all lead up to a podium that looks two-dimensional, next to which stands a plastic American flag on a pole. Running along the right side of the pews is a brown plastic room divider. A partition. This, you realize, is where Murphy & Milliken's holds wakes.

You were Meeker in *Inherit the Wind* in Ms Sline's class, the sweeping bailiff at the Hillsboro Courthouse whose words have always stayed with you: 'Matthew Harrison Brady . . .' you recall. 'I seen him once. At a Chautauqua meeting in Chattanooga,' and this you say out loud, it's your favorite line, and how you drove your mother *crazy* saying it, you remember, over and over: '. . . a Chautauqua meeting in Chattanooga,' which came right before 'The tent poles shook! *Who's gonna be your lawyer, son?*' – and you stop.

Because this, it's what Greg Tampico said to you *the night that you met,* as he was loosening his tie in the foyer of his walk-up, and you suddenly start imagining scenarios: like Greg Tampico is *here,* and he is going to pop out from behind the partition and go, like, *surprise* or more likely *hey, dummy;* or, like, Tampico is going to do something bigger, like pop out of a coffin or something (*ta-da*); and you can so totally picture Tampico, like, *hang gliding* into the parking lot of Murphy & Milliken's, but all you really *want* him to do is quietly open the doors, enter into this silent room, and creep up behind you on this wall-to-wall carpeting, and you can almost *feel* his broad chest pressing your shoulder blades now, his breath wet and warm on the back of your neck, when the eight lamps that hang down from the ceiling in pairs are turned on with a *click* –

'Greg,' you say, and face the doors.

It's not Greg Tampico. It's a janitor, a vacuum in one hand, and around the other, the long vacuum cord is festooned. His nametag says MARLEN.

'Can I help you,' he says.

Marlen, not fat but wide-middled, displays crooked, nut-colored teeth and these awful peaked eyebrows that make him look shocked. Marlen likely never made it past high school, you estimate (this is the part of your job you are really good at), but most definitely has a family, maybe a son or two, full-grown with wives pregnant, and though you are maybe just ten years apart, in one glance you can see the whole future cut of Marlen, the outline and mold of the old man he's on the cusp of becoming, and all this plant needs is a bit more sun and water, a bit more weathering of the skin, more ash in the hair, but he is *well* on his way, and his sudden appearance in the room, belt gripping his middle, ring of keys jangling a bad song off his hip, quite frankly makes you feel as though you've been cast into a boat departing the world of the living, and his vacuum's the oar.

As for you, you gauge quickly, it is likely that you appear to Marlen to be a young man too handsome to be trusted, one who's never held in his life what Marlen would call 'a real job.' For based on the look of your clothes, your hair, and the way you hold your shoulders back from your chest as you do, as though bearing wings; the way you are standing with your weight on one leg, shirtsleeves neatly rolled, the creamy flanks of your forearms unmarred by arm-hair (yes, you wax), you must be vain, *too vain* you are guessing he's guessing, to be of any real use to anyone, and it is likely that you work in finance or sales.

'I'm fine,' you say, thanking him in a manner that indicates *you're all set*.

But Marlen, like others you have met of his ilk, is not, and will never be, so summarily dismissed.

'Not supposed to be in here,' he says. 'Parlor's *closed*,' and he professionally winds the cord in a loop, hand to elbow.

You grin, showing off your white teeth. You walk toward him. You stick out your hand, turning it on: 'I'm so sorry,' you say. 'Nice to meet you. I'm Congressman Alexander Paine Wilson, First District,' and when you say this, the guy's wacky eyebrows smooth out.

'Voted for you,' he says, matter-of-factly. 'Me and my wife, we both did. Whole family's in Manassas.'

'I appreciate it,' you say, and wait for Marlen to say something right back, but Marlens never say something back. They have spoken so little in life that their rhythm's all wrong. '*Thanks a lot*,' you say once more, awkwardly splitting air. 'It's Marlen, right?'

'Pronounced Mar-*len*,' he says, like he's half Mark and half Leonard. 'Not like Brando.'

'Good to meet you,' you say. 'I'm here for the two o'clock service, but I'm early.'

'It's Monday,' he says.

'The two o'clock service,' you say. 'Today is Monday. Is that right?'

'Two clock –' Marlen says, and his head suddenly rips back, his mouth opening and his throat gagging like he's either trying to speak a word he's not accustomed to using or swallow something that got lodged there at lunch. His dry eyes squint. It goes on for far longer than comfortable, so long that you worry Marlen is, as Barb Newberg likes to say, *a few french fries short of a Happy Meal*, and you don't know if you liked him better when you thought he was your adversary instead of your ally, and are sort of appalled when his eyes actually roll and he chokes a little and swallows, working out whatever ailment just visited him.

'– been pushed to *three*,' he says, and points at the partition. 'Fellow's in there already, though. Don't know if there will be a priest,' he says, and when you ask why not, Marlen smirks. 'Fellow played for the *pink* team,' he says, and it's the way Marlen has said 'fellow' twice that's made his dumb politeness go mean. That super stale line about the 'pink team,' it makes you angry, worried that something more's come out in the news, something intimate maybe about you and Tampico, or even just Tampico himself, but you have no reason to worry: Marlen only watches TV from when he gets home until bed, then reads a bit of the Bible. He does not, you are guessing, own, like, a real phone. He's talking to you like he knows you, *because he voted for you he knows you,* thinks that while he wouldn't seek you out as a buddy, you'd fit in *just fine* with the other lightweights at his wife's church or something – and it's true that Marlen has every right to assume what he assumes as you have a super long record of Opposing Equality; received a 0% Human Rights rating in your first term from the ACLU; vote regularly to roll back existing protections for people of varying sexual orientations; opposed the repeals of Don't Ask, Don't Tell; toed the line during the long, vocal battle for DOMA; and even now are having your staffers write at length about your support for an amendment to the Constitution banning gay marriage (and abortion) for good in *Plaine Truth* – and whenever pressed to further address *why* you don't support the freedom to marry, especially now, when it's *law*, you just shrug and say, dumbly, and with the requisite intransigence compelled by your Party, some laws were meant to be *changed back*.

Because you'd rather not get into it with Marlen in the exact same way that you'd rather not get into it with anyone. Because, like, you are Not Gay, and how many times must you say it? And you don't appreciate it when your staffers tell you to stop posing *so gay* in pictures, and stop dressing *so gay* in your cowboy outfit just like the one Reagan wore, and stop combing your hair that old-fashioned way that's *so gay*, and stop laughing *so gay*, shaking hands *so gay*, smiling with a tilt of your head *so gay*, and you've worked pretty hard to fight this, and you even had photographers follow you once, into a gym, to photograph you doing something 'manly,' and you were, like, *lifting weights in a tank top, showing your guns*, and what could be more manly than that? You have no idea why everyone singles *you* out all the time when there are *plenty* of people you know, people in

· 147 ·

positions much more powerful than yours, who vote one way in public and live another in private, and it's hard to blame them; like you, they do not see themselves as hypocrites, they have simply seen *how America works,* have seen the oily machine of her power, and their desire to be included, to be a part of her Greatness, is so strong that they will create for themselves an Image.

It's been happening since the beginning of time. People like you who give no value to memory, who no longer imagine nor dream, should have evolved into something else a long time ago, but you've somehow endured *without evolving;* you make no sense and yet you are infinite, everlasting – and if you're really going to go here, as you apparently are, you can drag it all the way back to Alan Brickmann's marshmallow dick.

You always dated girls, but in seventh grade, there was Steve Marcini. In eighth, Parker Colson, Jimmy Bender. In ninth, tenth, eleventh, there was the fat kid, Sam Levenson (when he broke it off, that's when you punched him), and in twelfth, and even while at home from college, there was Chuck Myers, and you carried a thing for Chuck Myers through college, until senior year when you heard Chuck got married and you kind of went bananas and stopped tracking last names, sometimes even first names, and although you are Not Gay, there have always been men, young men, handsome even if they were not handsome, and it was only when you found yourself in your twenties in DC, clerking for a Republican congressman, when a woman walked by and was like *Has anyone ever told you you look like Ronald Reagan?* that the way forward made itself known: you became Ronald Reagan. And so to gay rights? Human rights?

Look at your hair, coal-black and coiffed. Look at your cheeks, nose and jawline. Your closet is full of shiny men's loafers, pastel summer sweaters, blazers with thick, padded shoulders, brass buttons. Look at your endless striped ties. You, you faggot, are an *aardvark,* an irrational, everlasting Earth-product, and whether you are ready to accept this or not, you have been, all this time, it must be said, wearing the skins of your enemy.

'If you want a peek, go ahead,' Marlen says. 'You won't *believe* what they do with 'em. I half expect 'em to wake up, come to life like Lazarus,' he says, haha.

'Who's Lazarus,' you say, because even Marlen, with his Bible, reads more than you do.

Marlen shakes his head at you. You *are* a politician, he's thinking. Unlike you, he's got *real-world experience,* he knows more than you do about *the world,* about *life,* he's got the Bible and he's got *street smarts,* and Marlen talks to himself as he leaves the room, vacuum in hand, as though you don't deserve to hear what he says, but you with your incredible hearing catch him answering your question out loud from behind the closed doors:

'Jesus brought him back from the dead! Resurrected him! Brought him out of his cave. *And Jesus said unto them, "Take off the grave clothes and let him go . . ."'*

You are not ready to View Greg Tampico. This all could still be some kind of joke or some accident, you think. Like, maybe the wake Marlen is talking about is not Greg Tampico's wake, *you don't know,* but all at once you do *not* want Greg Tampico to be behind the room divider.

Because if Greg Tampico is not behind the room divider, it means Vicky was right; it means Greg Tampico gave you the aardvark to get you to feel what you are feeling (*love*); to get you to realize that a public life in the private sector with Greg Tampico is a far, *far* better prospect than a private life in the public sector without Greg Tampico, and seriously now, like, *all you need* is for Greg Tampico to come up behind you, place his hands over your eyes and say what he said after you fled his apartment, that which you overheard on the stairwell through his weeping: 'You're so *blind*, you're so fucking *blind*,' and while you thought at the time that he was talking to himself, cursing himself, you understand now that he was cursing *you*, and Alex Wilson, it is true, you have been so fucking blind.

You walk over to the partition, grab the handles, and the whole wall accordions open.

∽

Thin Titus Downing returns from The Green Otter politely drunk off one beer, arms loaded with victuals, as the arc of sun crosses each of the twelve heads of stags like the hands of a priest. The lines are gone, no one peers into his windows. Outside, only the theater troupe remains.

The boys, beginning to feel the first waves of their hangovers, are collapsed on Downing's front step, and their throats are parched, their faces sunburned and weary. They are waiting for Downing to return so he will pay them and they can stay drunk. Their knees are dirty, their arms link, they've long lost their claws, but their heads, still donning papier-mâché pig noses, sway slightly as they hiccup through sloppy, sober harmonics, *'Phyllis is* (hic) *my only* (hic) *joy,'* and so this is the tune that Downing is absentmindedly whistling as he amiably walks through them and enters his shop, where noted prosthetic specialist Harold Skinner, his old roommate, is waiting.

'My friend,' Downing says. 'How'd we do.'

Skinner's neatly clipped handlebar is flat, soaked in sweat. 'Well, I did sell it,' he says.

'For how much?' Downing asks.

'Not much, I'm afraid. A German bought it.'

'A *German*?' says Downing, and he looks longingly at the table where the aardvark was stationed but now is gone.

He collapses into the chair where Rebecca Ostlet sat and listens in a daze as Skinner tells him how she was there the whole time, how there were no other women who entered the shop because the boys drove them off. How people didn't stay long – but it was only because it was so frightfully *hot* out, Skinner says, so Downing should not feel badly.

And Skinner explains, very gently, how the Gentlemen couldn't see the value in the aardvark, but Walter Potter, who would know, loved it. Called it a masterpiece.

'It *is* a masterpiece,' says Titus Downing.

'There's more,' Skinner says, and goes on to tell Titus Downing about the dogs: how Lady Ostlet, Mr Potter and Mr Skinner had all followed the Brontës upstairs to his private bedroom and found – what they found. And though Harold Skinner knows Downing perhaps better than most, he reminds him, as he spent two years living with him in a small room at Oxford and is entirely aware of the 'preference' of Titus Downing, aware what little interest Downing *ever* showed in female courtship, the sight of a naked blind man in Titus Downing's canopied bed *did* shock him, he admits.

'Rebecca dressed Richard,' Skinner says, 'and led him outside to her carriage,' and they both are, he guesses, at this moment probably, on the train back to London, discussing the new pair of prosthetic eyes which he, Harold Skinner, will, when he himself returns to London, design and craft.

Skinner only withholds from Downing the sorry picture he guesses the taxidermist himself can imagine: how, once Rebecca had loaded her husband into the carriage, he made no apologies, nor told her he loved her, but conveyed, in his way, what was expected of her from here on out. How Skinner had watched Rebecca cradling Richard's bandaged head in one of her arms, telling him something like *All will be well, dear, don't worry about a thing* and *Shush, dear, don't worry,* but what Skinner cannot know, and therefore cannot withhold, is that Rebecca Ostlet attended, on her own without Downing, the John Turtle Wood lecture at the Royal Institution on the remains of the Temple of Artemis at Ephesus.

There, she met a young, unattractive-but-funny civil engineer, and she and the unattractive-but-funny civil engineer, they have been seeing each other regularly, they have plans for marriage, and Rebecca is, in fact, newly pregnant – but now that's all gone to rot. England's divorce laws, though better than before, are still *bad for women,* and it is *so not lost* on Rebecca Ostlet that men have spent centuries arguing over the souls of the beasts while paying no heed to the souls of women, and Rebecca can only divorce Richard if she can prove his adultery, but his adultery, it must be said, is *not of the common kind* – any public revelation would be, she knows, universally ruinous – so it is quite clear to Rebecca as she departs Leamington Spa with her blind husband and the Brontës how her remaining years must be spent:

There are herbs, the botanist knows, such as barberry, ergot, coltsfoot and calomel. There is aloe and celery, black cohosh and hellebore, there is snakeweed, but the best course, she surmises, is likely the pennyroyal, the tansy or savin, abortifacients which can be procured at the pharmacist's, surreptitiously packaged as Beecham's Pills, as Farrer's Catholic Pills, as Hardy's Woman's Friend or Lydia Pinkham's Vegetable Compound, and there are Madame Drunette's Lunar Pills, Old Dr Gordon's 'Pearls of Health,' and if none of those work – Skinner cannot know that Rebecca Ostlet is thinking – she could risk arrest, in search of a 'flushing' for fifty guineas. Or she could just take a controlled fall down the stairs –

'I see,' Titus Downing says, and reaches quietly for his wallet. He pays Harold Skinner. He thanks him for his time and collects the German's pitiful receipt.

Skinner looks at his old friend and pauses at the front door. 'I can stay the night if you wish,' he says.

Downing assures him he's fine. That he prefers to be alone, but says again, 'Thank you,' as Skinner departs. Then Downing pays the theater troupe, tips them the wicker basket he carried home from The Green Otter. The duck and beans have congealed, but the bottles of wine are received with glee, and Downing lingers for a moment on his step, watching the boys rip off their costumes, once again link their arms, and take turns tugging from the bottles as they skip toward the Leam.

The yellow sun is going orange. The river is moving. The boys are dancing, singing as they go, *Yet she never fails to please, yet she never fails to please,* and Downing closes the front door with a sleigh jingle. He locks it.

The eyes of all stuffed creatures follow him as he walks through his workshop, past the black furry skin of the unfinished Schipperke, and he is breathing in slowly the stink of the Bengal tiger skin. All has been abandoned. All is quiet. Hot, summery fumes of clay, of musk and vinegar, of arsenical soaps, of red pepper and tannin and bisulfite of lime hang heavy in the air. Above it all, the rosemary musk of camphor.

Titus Downing walks to the table where he arranged the skin of the aardvark and unseals a glass bottle. White pills tumble into his palm like little teeth, and he carries them upstairs, into his bedroom, where the artist lies down on his bed, where the warm, meat-scent of Richard Ostlet's body is a ghost on the sheets.

∽

Enter the coffin. The lights of the Viewing area behind the partition have not yet been turned on, but when the room divider divides, it reveals a great big shiny coffin, black and boxy, reminding you at once of your Tahoe. You place your hands on the wood and feel a shock of cold, like it's been cut from a tree made of ice, and wonder what kind of wood the coffin is made of, and you cannot know that it is something called 'Leadwood,' *Combretum imberbe*, one of the strongest woods on Earth, nor that it has been imported all the way from Namibia – but whatever it is, you think, the lid is heavy, requires two hands to lift it, and as you lift it, the rosemary musk stinking up the whole funeral parlor rises out from inside, and the word enters your consciousness: *camphor*, and you know that it's camphor because Ms Sline made you do a science project examining the role of camphor in the death of cockroaches, and you (or your ten-year-old self) put five roaches into a jar, poked holes in the tin lid, dropped in a white pill of camphor and watched as, over the course of two days, the roaches, one by one, turned onto their backs, arched their spindly legs into the air, and died.

Other than the cockroaches, you have never seen a dead body before, not up close, not in person, and while Greg Tampico's body is certainly dead, there is also something strangely undead about it.

Looking at the body, you think, is exactly like looking at the body of a freaking department store *mannequin*.

The face, thank god, has been covered. The eyes have been wrapped tightly in a tear of white cloth that resembles a bandage, and you wager the funeral parlor has done this for reasons you don't want to think about but help-lessly do: like maybe the rims of the eyelids have been glued shut, are still *glistening wetly,* it's the reason for the delay, and by three o'clock the lids will have dried, the ban-dage may be removed – so you're relieved that the eyes are covered, wrapped up, because you definitely do not need to see them, those two blue globes which always seemed to grow wide, bulbous, whenever Greg Tampico saw you climbing the stairs of his walk-up, you know them already, every nuance of their color, their glassy sheen, you have stared into them for hours, countless *hours,* you realize, and staring into them always made you feel as though you actually belonged to something big, bigger than *you,* and you know that Greg Tampico, he felt the same way because one night you were both resting in each other's arms, smoking cigarettes in his bed, admiring the stuffed aard-vark, when he looked at you and said, all solemn, 'Weird, I've got *déjà vu,*' and you recall how dumb he sounded at the time, how you poked his guts with a sharp finger and snorted, *dork* or something, and he said, 'No really, I swear to god, we've been here before,' which is exactly what you're thinking while standing next to this body.

How lazy is the embalmer at Murphy & Milliken's who must not be paid a penny more than the minimum wage. Who clearly spent not, like, *a second more* than the minimum of time washing the body in some kind of cheap disinfectant before shaving the face, securing the jaw with some kind of wire before draining all blood from the veins and replacing it with some kind of crazy formaldehyde; how the hair was washed and pulled all to one side with a comb (precisely the manner in which it was *never* worn); how the ashen skin has been masked with a tan-colored paste sloppily wiped over the hands, neck and face, covering the pores of this cold meat that you once knew as 'Greg Tampico,' but the *color* is wrong, it's much too pale for the man who always sported a wrinkled tan from the Namibian sun; how the body's whole angle in repose, it looks *forced,* there is just something, like, *off* about it, and while you can guess that the embalmer does this with all bodies to try and make them look *restful* or *peaceful* — it's what the pillows are for — nothing about Greg Tampico's body looks right.

Although the body wears a full-dress tuxedo, the one he wore when you met, the way the broad shoulders have been tucked into silk cushions, the way the hands are folded, left over right as though their owner were religious and not apostate, the way the head has been tilted, ever so slightly to the right, as though to welcome Viewers for the Viewing, is flat-out *nothing* like the way the actual Greg Tampico gazed at you from his bed pillows, and though you do not know — and will never know — the word '*jiva,*' it's the word you are searching for: whatever the taxidermist captured so well in the aardvark has not *nearly* been captured in the body of Greg Tampico, and so you experience the peculiar feeling while you are looking at the body of Greg Tampico that this, at the same time, is not Greg Tampico at all. It's a nightmare.

You close the lid of the coffin.

You feel like you might cry, so you take out your phone. You sit down on a pew. You now have 18709 unread text messages and 24002 unread emails. You're being sub-poenaed. A congressional committee's about to be formed.

Scrolling through emails and text messages is what calms you, you are strangely calm, the roar of the media no longer troubles you, and it's like the calm of a blind man who has at long last been given sight but realizes there is nothing to see; or maybe it's like this guy Lazarus who, once he came out of his cave and Jesus wasn't there because he was, like, *done with him,* must have realized there was not much more to do other than go on unceremoniously living, because after the miracle's over, well, *then* what?

You feel this way, reading your emails, until you reach the part about who will be investigating you, and your phone nearly slips – movie-like – from your palms.

The leader of the committee who will be investigating the aardvark and who will, in a matter of weeks, uncover a host of financial improprieties, impeachable offenses, all, is none other than Representative William 'Billy' Rutledge (D).

∽

'What *happened*,' Downing had asked Ostlet last night.

It began with the aardvark. The night the hunter returned to camp with the aardvark, he left it on the ground to bleed out when he saw a light on in Richard's tent. 'It was late when he entered,' Ostlet said. 'No one knew he was there, and I was lying down with a wet cloth pressing my eyes.' When the hunter said he had some-thing to show him, Ostlet had apologized. Removed the compress. 'Not now,' he said. 'My eyes are killing me.'

The hunter, bone-thin but strong, knelt down next to him. 'I'm a doctor,' he said.

'I'm fine,' said Ostlet, but did not protest when the hunter took the compress from him, nor when he placed a hand over his eyes.

That's when, Ostlet told Downing, the hunter began moving his other hand down Ostlet's plump British figure, unbuttoned his trousers and softly explained to him how Nature is not criminal; how *common* it was for certain African men on expedition to engage in what might be called 'reciprocal sex'; how it was *common* for these men to declare more love for their boy-wives than their girl-wives, and why wouldn't Sir Richard Ostlet, the hunter said, *allow himself*, as such, to no longer feel pain? – and that was the moment, Ostlet explained, when he realized he loved Downing, that what he had *always* felt for Downing was love, and Ostlet begged Downing's forgiveness, but how could he possibly have known any sooner when there was no *language* to describe how he felt, no *currency*, and to even *attempt* to speak of it would have smacked of revolt, but a hopeless revolt, one toward a freedom that Ostlet knew did not exist – for Britain, didn't Downing know, was perfectly content to ignore them so long as there remained *ambiguity*, and hadn't Downing grown up reading, as Ostlet had, for decades, about the thousands of souls who tried to love one another *unambiguously*, or those who *got caught* and were tried all over England at the courts of assize, the quarter sessions and – hung? Was Downing so *thick* as to be unaware of the Offences Against the Person Act, and risk the both of them landing locked up for years, as men were, in Reading Gaol?

The hunter had held his swaying cock like it was a baby chick.

'Nature,' Ostlet said the hunter had said, as he began to work him, 'unlike Man, does nothing in vain. God is Nature, and because God is Nature, he created nothing in vain. Therefore, the soul can never expire. It is immortal and in perpetual transit.'

'The next morning,' Ostlet continued, 'the hunter showed me the aardvark, and I was feeling god-awful. It was brutally hot out. My eyes felt as though they might disengage completely, and the pain was, I must say, intolerable.' He explained to Downing how looking at the large dead aardvark had filled him with melancholy, for the aardvark, for himself, for Downing, for all this bloody *wasted time*, but how there was also beauty. He remembered what the hunter had said the previous evening, and the idea of what was possible began to take shape:

'That night I awoke and took camphor and whiskey – but not to die,' he said, 'just to numb myself for the procedure,' and early the next morning, after the hunter told everyone that Sir Richard was dead, leaving them to their sorrow, he returned to his own tent, far away from the British tents, where Ostlet, half-conscious, awaited him.

'The hunter stuck a small rod of iron into a fire, then severed and burned my ocular nerve bundles. The man,' Ostlet told Downing, 'literally cut the eyes out from my head. Put them into a jar of some kind of glycerin and formaldehyde – the hunter's "own preservative solution," or so he said – and then he put the jar into my specimen cabinet.'

The aardvark was sent, via Ostlet's assistant, to Titus Downing. The cabinet, unfortunately and quite by accident, went to Rebecca Ostlet.

'I stayed in Africa with the hunter a while longer to recover,' Ostlet said, and he ordered the construction of a coffin, a *sealed* coffin, to be sent back to London, as proof of his death.

'What was *in* it,' said Downing.

'The coffin was empty,' said Ostlet. 'But when it arrived in London, it was believed by all *not* to be empty,' and went on to explain that the wood used to build it was an extremely heavy African wood, a unique *Combretum imberbe* known to exist only in southern Africa under the common name Leadwood, and it is a tree which can live for a thousand years, the hunter told him, and the Herero and the Namaqua, they all worship the tree, as to them Leadwood is the great healer, a shared ancestor of Animal and Man.

'When I was well enough,' he said, 'I returned first to London, to Gloucester Walk. I had rather hoped to catch a moment when Rebecca was *out* of the house, so I could go *in* – so I might save Rebecca from opening the cabinet, from finding my –' and there Richard stopped short. 'But she *never* left,' he said. And though he walked by their flat several times, widows, he knew, they could grieve for *a full year,* never leaving home, and so Ostlet, upon hearing the bark of the Brontës whenever he passed, upon smelling the roses which filled their flat, assumed she had returned to her botany, become a rosarian and was perfectly content, and about this, Downing did not correct him.

'But *why*,' Downing asked. 'Why do it?'

'The pain, you see,' said Ostlet, and he reached blindly for Downing's thin waist. 'I could no longer *bear it* –'

'Dickie,' Titus heard himself whisper, and he touched the bandage wrapped around his lover's face.

'It's me,' Richard said, and the two men grabbed each other's forearms.

And Downing grinned, weeping, and Ostlet opened his own mouth and, in his way, wept, knowing now that as everyone believed he was dead, they could at long last *live*, retire to Downing's farm in Northumberland as Downing always had dreamed, and from here on out *all things were possible*, and all they needed do now was sell the gigantic taxidermied aardvark for the highest possible sum –

Exit the aardvark, enter the evening. It is August. Enter a warm, passing breeze through a window left open as Titus Downing sits up in his canopied bed. His hand holding the camphor, it throbs. The scar, he observes, looks like half a halo. He is forty-one years old.

After Ostlet explained what had happened, Downing, comforted believing that souls are not destroyed at death, not merely created and then destroyed but infinitely *transferred, passed on*, waited until his lover was sleeping, then crept downstairs, into his workshop. There he stood in his dressing gown in front of his battered pine workbenches, his rows of glass bottles of salt of tartar, of palm wine.

He removed the cloth bag from its nail on the wall and selected the piercing awl. He went to the aardvark.

Tipping her on one side, he carefully etched under the mount made of Leadwood, deep in the grain, a good luck symbol, a little hooked cross, the Hindu symbol for the nature of the machine of the universe, for how the *jiva* cycles peacefully on, into infinity.

How many lives have I already lived, Downing wonders, undressing himself. He folds his clothes neatly in squares, as though the clothes are a body he wears for one season, removes for the next. If his soul will never expire, the next season will simply bring, the taxidermist thinks as he ingests the camphor pills, one by one, more of the same.

Whatever comes next will be nothing more than a new arrangement of skin.

∿

'When you can't make them see the light,' Ronald Reagan famously said, 'make them feel the heat,' and it's the quote Rutledge spoke upon seeing *Images of Greatness* adorning your coffee table the first time.

Enter Rutledge, six months ago, into your townhouse. Enter, like you, a young and handsome upcoming congressman, amply-muscled and blond, who quoted Ronald Reagan the day he met you, destabilizing you into trusting him despite the fact that he was a Democrat. Enter Rutledge, who once told you, shaking his head sympathetically, that he's known Nancy Beavers since Georgetown and you'd 'better look out 'cuz she's tough as nails.'

While you had presumed Rutledge had left three days ago for his vacation at his farmhouse with his wife and five sons while Congress was not in session, clearly Rutledge was *not at the fucking farmhouse*; Rutledge was trolling 2486 Asher Place, *watching you* in a way that you did not know you were being watched – and it could have been, like, as recent as *last week* over lite beers and peanut butter sandwiches and Scrabble in your kitchen that Rutledge casually told Olioke about an address you often visited on King Street in Alexandria, an address belonging to the name 'Gregory Tampico,' and, by chance, did Olioke know this Tampico guy?

Of course Olioke knew him. Gregory Tampico and Solomon Olioke (you flat-out, hands-down, like, *seriously fucking hate Olioke*), they shared *Namibia,* and Olioke attended many Happiness Foundation fundraisers, and how many times across ballrooms, across tables all adorned with English bone china, across glittering chandeliers and candles as lukewarm chicken piccata and some kind of scampi were served, *how many times* did you see Olioke standing there in the corner, expressionless as a coatrack?

You have no friends. You are hemorrhaging alliances. Greg Tampico is dead. Your mother doesn't like you. Toby Castle doesn't like you. Even Olioke, a fellow Republican, has thrown you under the bus for Nancy Fucking Beavers's fucking stooge Rutledge, but the reason why is inexplicable until you remember: *the aardvark*. Olioke *knew* Tampico had it.

After Tampico gave notice, quit directing the foundation, Olioke must have wanted to *return it*, you think, *to his people,* and *really,* he, like, could have just taken the aardvark and made off with it somehow, leaving you out of it, but *no* – Nancy Beavers would be 'super grateful,' Rutledge told Olioke, and when the time came, as everyone knew it eventually would, she 'would *not forget* about the good people of Rhode Island' – and as you make for the exit of Murphy & Milliken's, absorbing how it played out, the irony of your reelection campaign missive 'Divide to unite' is *so* not lost on you. It becomes clear how, together, Republican and Democrat united, Rutledge and Olioke *spied on you and Greg Tampico*.

How they must have sat in a dark car outside Tampico's walk-up. How, after you fled Greg Tampico's the last time you saw him, it must have been Rutledge and Olioke who followed the medics who came spilling out of the ambulance when Tampico's landlady found him. How the two of them must have stood over the zebra-pelt bedspread after the body was removed, discussing what to do until Rutledge, he said he had an idea: *Olioke* could contact your staffers about Greg Tampico's death and *Rutledge* could borrow a FedEx uniform, a FedEx truck and a clipboard, all for fifty dollars in cash, from a pair of heroin addicts working this remote FedEx place he knew. And *Olioke* nicked one piece of Tampico's gilded letterhead from the messy stack which he always kept on the imitation Louis XIV French dresser, next to the aardvark, assembled both the blank note and the aardvark into a large brown packing box, loaded her up onto the FedEx truck, and then *Rutledge*, wearing fake eyeglasses, some crazy fake beard, a FedEx uniform, trusting that you never look long or hard at anything except mirrors, *delivered her* right *to you* at the front door of 2486 Asher Place yesterday morning –

You have no proof. But all of this you know in your bones to be true, and six weeks from now, when you are seated in front of the congressional committee for your various crimes, it is why you will look right into Representative Rutledge's eyes and apologize. Say that you have no memory of the FedEx man who delivered the aardvark other than what small details you share. No memory at all.

Outside the funeral home, it is a hot blue American day. Cars have begun to enter the roundabout, and out from them spill strangers, black people and white people, young and old, who all knew Greg Tampico, who liked and loved him, and they are dressed simply, respectfully, in black suits and black dresses, they all seem to know each other – through tears, they embrace – until enter the florist with bushels of flowers, you have no idea what kind, they are yellow and white, they're going inside by the armload as more people arrive with the food, a huge spread of what looks and smells like some kind of African fare, and someone else is unloading a large funeral guest book, a cheap gilded sign for out front that just sounds wrong: CELEBRATING THE COMPLETED LIFE OF GREGORY ALLEN TAMPICO.

You do not participate. You climb into the Tahoe, which won't be yours for long. You close the door.

And here is where you sit, your hands gripping the wheel, your forehead resting on top of them for *thirty-two minutes,* the amount of time it will take for the paparazzi and Officer Anderson and Brian Castle to find you, and you sitting here, alone in the Tahoe in the parking lot of a budget funeral parlor in Alexandria, Virginia, with your head on your hands as though privately sobbing, *this* will be the final broadcasted image of your undoing, and my god, what will you think when you see yourself in such a state on TV, as you most certainly will? Or, like, when the *memes* all start coming like they came for Keanu eating lunch on that bench, and they will say SAD FASCIST IS SAD or SAD ALEX WILSON IS THE NEW SAD KANYE IS THE NEW SAD KEANU, or you will appear to be weeping over a volleyball which has been photoshopped onto your lap: *WIIILSON!*

But they're wrong. As you sit here, waiting for the world to descend, you are not sobbing. You are wondering what they have done with the aardvark.

The last time you saw her, she was in your Tahoe and Olioke was in the kitchen, making himself a peanut butter sandwich with his rust-dotted paring knife, waiting for you to turn on the TV upstairs, and the moment he heard your TV go on, he must have put down the knife and walked through your living room. He must have opened the door to your garage, where, when he turned on the light, there must have stood Rutledge, waiting at the back of the Tahoe.

And Rutledge embraced the aardvark by her mount, lifting her as though she weighed nothing at all (he benches 280), then carried her upstairs to the kitchen, stashed her under your custom Calacutta Italian marble breakfast bar ($12487), and slipped, undetected, into his room as Olioke returned to the kitchen. And Olioke, he did not speak, or even move from his seat, when your bedroom door slammed shut, when you dashed through the living room, flew downstairs into the garage and backed the Tahoe out into the street to drive to Alexandria for Tampico's funeral this afternoon – Olioke was just waiting, calmly eating his sandwich at the sink, as you roared off toward Murphy & Milliken's, as all the reporters and paparazzi packed up their white vans and followed you, and at last, when everyone hád fled 2486 Asher Place, Rutledge only then emerged from his room and asked: 'Is he gone?'

Olioke picked up his phone.

Not five minutes later, you guess, two young women in tank tops and skinny jeans from Abercrombie arrived at the front door, and Olioke brought them inside. He embraced them, his family, his two eldest Namibian American daughters, Rheinhilde and Herlinde, and the latter urged, 'Hurry up, Dad, the flight leaves in three hours,' but no one seemed to particularly hurry as the aardvark was blanketed in bubble wrap, returned to the large cardboard box, taped up and sealed and delivered into Rutledge's 'borrowed' FedEx truck, which must have been – was – parked this whole time one block over, and which would carry the aardvark into the belly of an airplane leaving Dulles, which is where she is now.

The aardvark will travel via plane, taxi, flatbed truck, and another flatbed truck through four countries until she at last arrives in Olioke's great-grandparents' native village, not far at all from the place where she was rooted out from a tunnel late one night in 1875. But what is time.

The Herero, when they receive her, will not carry on or even mildly effuse; rather, donning their reappropriated

Victorian garb, the skins of their enemy, they will hoist her up onto their shoulders and parade her to a local and magnificent *Combretum imberbe*, what is called in Afrikaans *hardekool*, and the wood of the *hardekool* is very dense, very hard and termite resistant, and it is under the shade of the enormous Leadwood tree that the Herero will quietly, without fanfare, celebrate the aardvark's new season. Give her new life.

You are also about to be given a new life.

Months Later

'THE DISTRACTIONS OF CONSTANT questions impede my ability to serve the First District' is the official statement you offered after the first day of your hearing, which was supposed to go on for months but, once you resigned, was over. *WaPo* is reporting that federal investigators are still looking into your spending, have subpoenaed witnesses to appear before a grand jury next month – but your resignation prevents further inquiry from Congress.

The authorities seized your Ronald Reagan collection. (There was no comment from the Reagan family, though when the collection is mentioned, as it is occasionally mentioned on CNN, it is called 'creepy.') They seized your clothes. All of your assets. They seized the canary-yellow velvet Victorian sofa, at which point you suffered a particularly biting stab of depression and called your mother. You asked her for help, financial or otherwise, and all she said was what she usually says: 'You never wanted love, never at all,' so *that* was a mistake, and it's all how you find yourself renting this two-bedroom apartment in Silver Spring.

There is no light. Your new apartment is on the ground floor of an apartment complex with, you swear it, the exact same wall-to-wall as Murphy & Milliken's, and all windows face walls except the one offering a level view of a dirt courtyard. A waterlogged picnic table. The kitchen cabinets, they stick to your hands when you open them, and the place came furnished with bulk items, your new landlord cheerfully told you, straight out of Bob's Pit, and you cannot even remotely fathom what on earth he meant by 'Bob's Pit,' but you dare not go online to find out.

The place is cheap, with a mildewed bathroom, but it's a place to live. A place to figure out what to do next. It has an Insignia 24-inch Class flat-screen TV ($69.99) and free Wi-Fi.

Vicky's been on four times, *Oprah* through *Ellen*. He says when he grows up he wants to be a congressman . . . *or a clown!* and he really hams it up so everyone laughs each time he says *or a clown!*

Every night, dinner is Chinese from your local, a hole-in-the-wall called 'Fortune's Palace.' You eat at the coffee table in sweatpants, your eyes darting from the glow of your TV screen to the glow of your laptop, searching for news, and there used to be quite a bit of news about you – a guy you barely knew from way back in fifth grade, from Ms Sline's class, got some attention when he told Bill Maher, 'Look, *we* called him "Odd Fuck" –' aloud, on TV. Now there's less.

Nancy Fucking Beavers is not even talking about you;

she's *moved on,* she said months ago, and squeezed herself into a new butter-colored pantsuit for the campaign trail. 'It's better that America just *move on,*' she says, and our country is imperfect, she says, but better than any other at *fighting injustice,* and while she is serving the First District she will continue to fight injustice for the sake of our *children,* and how she leans on that word! Her neutered-looking husband, Cody Beavers, and their two moonfaced children, Bailey and Alicia, are pressed to her sides as Nancy talks about her revised platform, which is Family, but how Family is different for all people, and all people are different, it's what makes America *America,* and then her campaign song comes on, 'What Makes America America,' and you laugh because she doesn't know it's a slogan for Subarus, and Ole Beavers, you have to hand it to her, she really knows how to lean on those platitudes and has a 78% Favorability Rating – but right now it's all you can take.

You already know what the 2024 Democratic presidential ticket will be, the reason Rutledge rooted you out from your tunnel: Beavers-Rutledge. God help you.

You turn off the TV. You must stop waiting for something new to be said, or for something to happen. Because nothing will happen.

Besides, you have work tomorrow.

One person is still with you. Never left your side. Barb Newberg found you this apartment, a job at the Library of Congress, and it's where you've gone the past month.

You're in the Jefferson Building. You're what they call a 'minor researcher.' It's the sort of job usually reserved for recent college grads, and the only grown men you ever see there are these tired guys with hairlines in various degrees of distress who wear abominable short-sleeved oxford dress shirts from Van Heusen which they order on Amazon ($18.99), out of which swing their pale forearms.

These men, they appear trapped in time, their shirts tucked tightly into khakis with pleats at the front that are belted with braided leather, over which hang their soft middles. Black woolen socks are stuffed into cheap penny loafers sans pennies (due to forgetfulness or neglect, you really don't know), and the loafers have been worn for so long that the heels have gone slant, making them all walk sort of bowlegged. The way they shuffle and slide around the marble floors of the magnificent Jefferson Building they could, like, be in their *living rooms,* you think, a mug of chamomile tea somewhere at the ready, and they barely speak, and when they do speak, it's in veritable *whispers* – 'The men's needs more paper,' they wheeze – and they are not disagreeable; they are plain-spoken, uncurious, like they haven't been laid in a decade.

Women, it seems, are everywhere. It's clear they own the place, the way their voices echo like bossy birds around the library, and you hear them talking authoritatively about the state of the Reading Rooms, the state of their personal childcare, and they all wear clunky one-inch Mary Janes for the middle-aged set with shitty knees, their thighs pinch and bloom under too-tight slacks – slacks they might have gotten away with eight years ago but they cannot yet psychically commit themselves to the next size up – and tucked into the slacks are blouses of flimsy faux-silk, over which are draped lightweight buttoned sweaters of varying cuts, which they all wear to combat the relentless A/C, and their woman-backs are all fat, broad and down-turned, like someone's been sitting on their shoulders for years, their posture is terrible, and no matter how they try to accessorize, all the cheap earrings and necklaces and scarves do zero to hide the lumps of their figures, and you catch yourself staring sometimes at how *similar* the men all look but how *weirdly different* the women all are: how some balloon in the bellies, which look like covered bowls, and some balloon in the butts, which they constantly try to cover up with their sweaters that are always too short, and some even balloon on the sides – like the fat had nowhere else it might possibly go so it went to the *sides* – and when you stare at them in the way that you do, as if saying *oh sweetie*, they always look back at you in a collective expression of what appears to be a common recipe of pity and scorn.

Your reckoning comes in the shape of your boss, a good friend of Barb Newberg's, who goes by the name Marjorie Pinkwater.

Relatively speaking, Pinkwater is fit. She wears her hair short, which you've always disliked on women but it somehow suits Pinkwater, and she dresses sensibly but with a whiff of style: ironed slacks and those blouses that tie in the front, and she reminds you of a young Diane Keaton, Meryl Streep. But Pinkwater is serious, like Barb Newberg. She is good at her job, does not appreciate irony, and gives everyone Flextime.

In fact, you're not sure that anyone has ever put in a

full day's work here, the men and women all work primarily in five-hour shifts, and Pinkwater regularly hands out little colorful bags with soaps inside for people's birthdays, gift cards to Starbucks or a mysterious place called 'TJ Maxx,' and even though you've only worked here for a month, so far every Wednesday morning Pinkwater has arrived at the Library loaded up with Panera, giant plastic bins packed with bagels, with muffins and danish, which she leaves for everyone in the break room, and when you asked Pinkwater why, *why* so many pastries, she looked at you like you were nuts and said, 'Hump Day!'

This afternoon, Pinkwater is in the break room talking health care to everyone while spreading strawberry jam on a bagel. It's all in the news. She's pushing for better coverage for part-timers, she says, but no promises, and although you rarely speak in this place, at this new job, the way she talks so eagerly about expanding government prompts you to say:

'The nine most terrifying words in the English language are "I'm from the government and I'm here to help."'

It's Ronald Reagan. It just slipped out.

Pinkwater, knowing perfectly well who you are (or were), stops her spreading. She picks a congealed strawberry off her bagel, flicks it into the sink, and for some reason, you have no idea why, begins talking about her abortion in college. How she does not regret it. How it's one of the easiest procedures in the world actually, and Pinkwater has had monthly periods that were harder than her abortion, she says, and if you want to talk *big government*, how much *bigger*, how much more invasive and controlling can government get when it's allowed to patrol a freaking uterus? A safe abortion is *a basic right,* she says, *required for the full emancipation of women,* and guys like you, Alex Wilson, have ridden high on the backs of women's rights for too long, too long, she says, prompting the other women to nod their heads deeply. They chime in like, Pinkwater, we've *all* had abortions, and they all start in about their abortions.

'I was out in three minutes,' one says, and as they get into it, the women are so matter-of-fact that they scare you.

You glance around the room in a slight panic. Like *something is going on,* something is happening that you do not understand, because despite all that has happened to you, you still have not evolved, perhaps will never evolve –

Yet there is hope for you.

Because certain late nights, you have noticed, your apartment in Silver Spring is accompanied by certain strange noises. It's like someone outside is *walking the grounds* around your apartment building before pausing, for a moment, in front of your window, and despite the fact that you are on the ground floor and keep the blinds closed when you watch TV, you can, like, *totally discern* the *snap-shuck* of a Zippo.

You can, from within the confines of your living room, smell the burn of the cigarette, hear its little crisping fire followed by the deep, warm sigh of a man leaning his back against the Maryland brick, smoking, and Greg Tampico, he *always* used Zippos, he *always* sighed like that after the first drag, and while you understand intellectually that it cannot be Tampico, there's just no *way* that it's Tampico, the figure who has begun appearing outside your window late at night, smoking, strikes your imagination in such a way that it frightens you – your dreams, you're unaccustomed to using them – and on those nights, it feels as though Tampico's really *there,* with you even though he's not with you, and so this *ghost* is, like, *a starting point,* now *room has been made,* there is now a place within you where your imagination can take root and maybe grip you, maybe grow – and the Herero, the Namibians sporting the skins of their oppressor, they too are on your mind as you sit here in the break room of the Jefferson Building listening to Pinkwater, staring helplessly at the colorful rack of lightweight ladies' sweaters, the Costco mini fridge and microwave matching set, the coffee mugs that have been washed and carefully dried that say things like DANCE LIKE NOBODY'S WATCHING or EVERYTHING WHALE BE ALRIGHT (with a picture of a whale on it), or WOMEN'S PAIN IS NOT NECESSARY FOR MEN'S SELF-DISCOVERY, or the chintzy-ass poster of Thomas Jefferson on the wall above the sink and the quote beneath it – ACTION WILL DELINEATE AND DEFINE YOU – until you meet eyes with the only other man there on break.

He is sitting with you and the women at the table, but you didn't even notice him until now. He could be anywhere from forty to sixty, you think, and is, like, *completely at ease* with the conversation. He is helping himself to a lemon poppy-seed muffin big as a small cake, the biggest one in Pinkwater's bin. As his hand reaches for it, you can see a blue network of raised veins stretching toward his knuckles, it's the slow blood chugging in and out of his heart, and watching him reach for the muffin ignites something within you: it's like, you don't even *want* the muffin.

But it suddenly matters to you that you get it.

You are fast, faster than he is by a long shot, and because you want the muffin and you are fast, you can easily get the muffin first in a quick grab (which, to the tremulous shock of the man, you do), and it's even heavier than you expected, all almond oil, and you do not even bother to peel off the wrapper as you hold the muffin in front of your face and gaze at your new enemy. You *do* want this muffin, you are *hungry*, you think, and make a mental note to go on Amazon tonight to order your penny loafers. A week's worth of Van Heusen. A cheap braided belt. Khakis.

It's not the first time, you think, it won't be the last, and delightedly watch his wrinkled face fall as you take a large bite, bearing yourself into the infinite boredom.

Acknowledgments

This novel would be invisible were it not for the honesty and talents of Jim Rutman. I am also deeply grateful for the overwhelming generosity and incisive queries of my brilliant editor, Jean Garnett, and for the extraordinary support of Reagan Arthur and everyone at Little, Brown, notably Betsy Uhrig and Dianna Stirpe. Across the pond, I thank Kirsty Dunseath, my editor at Penguin Random House UK, for her assistance with all things British. With further gratitude to Ethan Nosowsky, Deb Olin Unferth and the Creative Capital Foundation, the Maine Arts Commission, the Bogliasco Foundation, the Anderson Center for the Arts, Bates College, and the Visitor Information Centre in Royal Leamington Spa, England. I must also thank Karol Frühauf and György Himmler for hiring me during the summer of 2017 to escape U.S. politics and guard the Maria Valeria Bridge between Štúrovo, Slovakia, and Esztergom, Hungary, and finish this book. Next, I thank Brian Brodeur, Benjamin Chadwick, Tracy Zeman, Courtney Campbell, Zachary Tyler Vickers, Paul X. Rutz, Thomas Israel Hopkins. Acknowledgments are further due to *Practical Taxidermy*, by Montagu Browne (1878); 'The Aard-Vark or Earth-Hog,' by Émile Oustalet

(1879); 'Biology of the Aardvark,' by Joachim Knöthig (2005); 'Thoughts out of Season on the History of Animal Ethics,' by Dr Rod Preece (2007); 'Bayle's "Rorarius," Liebniz and Animal Souls,' by Richard Fry (2015); 'Anthropomorphic Taxidermy and the Death of Nature,' by Michelle Henning (2007); *Reincarnation in World Thought,* by Joseph Head and S. L. Cranston (1967); and *Images of Greatness: An Intimate Look at the Presidency of Ronald Reagan,* by Pete Souza (2004). As we hurtle to the end, I thank Julie, my laugh machine and 'Insider,' and, of course, my greatest thanks go to the love of my life (and the next), JW.

About the Author

Jessica Anthony is the author of *The Convalescent*, and her writing has appeared in *Best New American Voices*, *McSweeney's*, and *New American Writing*. Anthony has been a butcher in Alaska, an unlicensed masseuse in Poland, a secretary in San Francisco. While writing *Enter the Aardvark*, Anthony was working as a 'Bridge Guard' on the Maria Valeria Bridge between Štúrovo, Slovakia, and Esztergom, Hungary. She lives in Maine, USA.